LITTLE HOUSE

LITTLE HOUSE
IN THE BIG WOODS

LITTLE HOUSE
IN THE BIG WOODS

by LAURA INGALLS WILDER

HarperTrophy®
An Imprint of HarperCollins*Publishers*

HarperCollins®, ☰®, Little House®, and The Laura Years™ are trademarks of HarperCollins Publishers.

Little House in the Big Woods

www.littlehousebooks.com

Library of Congress Catalog Card Number 52-7525
ISBN-10: 0-06-088537-8 (pbk.)
ISBN-13: 978-0-06-088537-3 (pbk.)

❖

First published in 1932
First Harper Trophy edition, 1971
Revised Harper Trophy edition, 2007

CONTENTS

LITTLE HOUSE
IN THE BIG WOODS

LITTLE HOUSE
IN THE BIG WOODS

Once upon a time, sixty years ago, a little girl lived in the Big Woods of Wisconsin, in a little gray house made of logs.

The great, dark trees of the Big Woods stood all around the house, and beyond them were other trees and beyond them were more trees. As far as a man could go to the north in a day, or a week, or a whole month, there was nothing but woods. There were no houses. There were no roads. There were no people. There were only trees and the wild animals who had their homes among them.

Wolves lived in the Big Woods, and bears, and huge wild cats. Muskrats and mink and otter lived by the streams. Foxes had dens in the hills and deer roamed everywhere.

To the east of the little log house, and to the west, there were miles upon miles of trees, and only a few little log houses scattered far apart in the edge of the Big Woods.

So far as the little girl could see, there was only the one little house where she lived with her father and mother, her sister Mary and baby sister Carrie. A wagon track ran before the house, turning and twisting out of sight in the woods where the wild animals lived, but the little girl did not know where it went, nor what might be at the end of it.

The little girl was named Laura and she called her father, Pa, and her mother, Ma. In those days and in that place, children did not say Father and Mother, nor Mamma and Papa, as they do now.

At night, when Laura lay awake in the trundle bed, she listened and could not hear anything at all but the sound of the trees whispering together. Sometimes, far away in the night, a wolf howled. Then he came nearer, and howled again.

It was a scary sound. Laura knew that wolves would eat little girls. But she was safe inside the solid log walls. Her father's gun hung over the door and good old Jack, the brindle bulldog, lay on guard before it. Her father would say:

"Go to sleep, Laura. Jack won't let the wolves in." So Laura snuggled under the covers of the trundle bed, close beside Mary, and went to sleep.

One night her father picked her up out of bed and carried her to the window so that she might see the wolves. There were two of them sitting in front of the house. They looked like shaggy dogs. They pointed their noses at the big, bright moon, and howled.

Jack paced up and down before the door, growling. The hair stood up along his back and he showed his sharp, fierce teeth to the wolves.

They howled, but they could not get in.

The house was a comfortable house. Upstairs there was a large attic, pleasant to play in when the rain drummed on the roof. Downstairs was the small bedroom, and the big room. The bedroom had a window that closed with a wooden shutter. The big room had two windows with glass in the panes, and it had two doors, a front door and a back door.

All around the house was a crooked rail fence, to keep the bears and the deer away.

In the yard in front of the house were two beautiful big oak trees. Every morning as soon as she was awake Laura ran to look out of the window, and one morning she saw in each of the big trees a dead deer hanging from a branch.

Pa had shot the deer the day before and Laura had been asleep when he brought them home at night and hung them high in the trees so the wolves could not get the meat.

That day Pa and Ma and Laura and Mary had fresh venison for dinner. It was so good that Laura wished they could eat it all. But most of the meat must be salted and smoked and packed away to be eaten in the winter.

For winter was coming. The days were shorter, and frost crawled up the window panes at night. Soon the snow would come. Then the log house would be almost buried in snow-drifts, and the lake and the streams would freeze. In the bitter cold weather Pa could not be sure of finding any wild game to shoot for meat.

The bears would be hidden away in their dens where they slept soundly all winter long. The squirrels would be curled in their nests in hollow trees, with their furry tails wrapped snugly around their noses. The deer and the rabbits would be shy and swift. Even if Pa could get a deer, it would be poor and thin, not fat and plump as deer are in the fall.

Pa might hunt alone all day in the bitter cold, in the Big Woods covered with snow, and come home at night with nothing for Ma and Mary and Laura to eat.

So as much food as possible must be stored away in the little house before winter came.

Pa skinned the deer carefully and salted and stretched the hides, for he would make soft leather of them. Then he cut up the meat, and sprinkled salt over the pieces as he laid them on a board.

Standing on end in the yard was a tall length cut from the trunk of a big hollow tree. Pa had driven nails inside as far as he could reach from each end. Then he stood it up, put a little roof over the top, and cut a little door on one side near the bottom. On the piece that he cut out he fastened leather hinges; then he fitted it into place, and that was the little door, with the bark still on it.

After the deer meat had been salted several days, Pa cut a hole near the end of each piece and put a string through it. Laura watched him do this, and then she watched him hang the meat on the nails in the hollow log.

He reached up through the little door and hung meat on the nails, as far up as he could reach. Then he put a ladder against the log, climbed up to the top, moved the roof to one side, and reached down inside to hang meat on those nails.

Then Pa put the roof back again, climbed down the ladder, and said to Laura:

"Run over to the chopping block and fetch me some of those green hickory chips—new, clean, white ones."

So Laura ran to the block where Pa chopped wood, and filled her apron with the fresh, sweet-smelling chips.

Just inside the little door in the hollow log Pa built a fire of tiny bits of bark and moss, and he laid some of the chips on it very carefully.

Instead of burning quickly, the green chips smoldered and filled the hollow log with thick, choking smoke. Pa shut the door, and a little smoke squeezed through the crack around it and a little smoke came out through the roof, but most of it was shut in with the meat.

"There's nothing better than good hickory smoke," Pa said. "That will make good venison that will keep anywhere, in any weather."

Then he took his gun, and slinging his ax

on his shoulder he went away to the clearing to cut down some more trees.

Laura and Ma watched the fire for several days. When smoke stopped coming through the cracks, Laura would bring more hickory chips and Ma would put them on the fire under the meat. All the time there was a little smell of smoke in the yard, and when the door was opened a thick, smoky, meaty smell came out.

At last Pa said the venison had smoked long enough. Then they let the fire go out, and Pa took all the strips and pieces of meat out of the hollow tree. Ma wrapped each piece neatly in paper and hung them in the attic where they would keep safe and dry.

One morning Pa went away before daylight with the horses and wagon, and that night he came home with a wagonload of fish. The big wagon box was piled full, and some of the fish were as big as Laura. Pa had gone to Lake Pepin and caught them all with a net.

Ma cut large slices of flaky white fish, without one bone, for Laura and Mary. They all feasted on the good, fresh fish. All they did not eat fresh was salted down in barrels for the winter.

Pa owned a pig. It ran wild in the Big Woods, living on acorns and nuts and roots. Now he caught it and put it in a pen made of logs, to fatten. He would butcher it as soon as the weather was cold enough to keep the pork frozen.

Once in the middle of the night Laura woke up and heard the pig squealing. Pa jumped out of bed, snatched his gun from the wall, and ran outdoors. Then Laura heard the gun go off, once, twice.

When Pa came back, he told what had happened. He had seen a big black bear standing beside the pigpen. The bear was reaching into the pen to grab the pig, and the pig was running and squealing. Pa saw this in the starlight and he fired quickly. But the light was dim and in his haste he missed the bear. The bear ran away into the woods, not hurt at all.

Laura was sorry Pa did not get the bear.

She liked bear meat so much. Pa was sorry, too, but he said:

"Anyway, I saved the bacon."

The garden behind the little house had been growing all summer. It was so near the house that the deer did not jump the fence and eat the vegetables in the daytime, and at night Jack kept them away. Sometimes in the morning there were little hoof-prints among the carrots and the cabbages. But Jack's tracks were there, too, and the deer had jumped right out again.

Now the potatoes and carrots, the beets and turnips and cabbages were gathered and stored in the cellar, for freezing nights had come.

Onions were made into long ropes, braided together by their tops, and then were hung in the attic beside wreaths of red peppers strung on threads. The pumpkins and the squashes were piled in orange and yellow and green heaps in the attic's corners.

The barrels of salted fish were in the pantry,

and yellow cheeses were stacked on the pantry shelves.

Then one day Uncle Henry came riding out of the Big Woods. He had come to help Pa butcher. Ma's big butcher knife was already sharpened, and Uncle Henry had brought Aunt Polly's butcher knife.

Near the pigpen Pa and Uncle Henry built a bonfire, and heated a great kettle of water over it. When the water was boiling they went to kill the hog. Then Laura ran and hid her head on the bed and stopped her ears with her fingers so she could not hear the hog squeal.

"It doesn't hurt him, Laura," Pa said. "We do it so quickly." But she did not want to hear him squeal.

In a minute she took one finger cautiously out of an ear, and listened. The hog had stopped squealing. After that, Butchering Time was great fun.

It was such a busy day, with so much to see and do. Uncle Henry and Pa were jolly, and there would be spare-ribs for dinner, and Pa had promised Laura and Mary the bladder and the pig's tail.

As soon as the hog was dead Pa and Uncle Henry lifted it up and down in the boiling water till it was well scalded. Then they laid it on a board and scraped it with their knives, and all the bristles came off. After that they hung the hog in a tree, took out the insides, and left it hanging to cool.

When it was cool they took it down and cut it up. There were hams and shoulders, side meat and spare-ribs and belly. There was the heart and the liver and the tongue, and the head to be made into headcheese, and the dishpan full of bits to be made into sausage.

The meat was laid on a board in the back-door shed, and every piece was sprinkled with salt. The hams and the shoulders were put to pickle in brine, for they would be smoked, like the venison, in the hollow log.

"You can't beat hickory-cured ham," Pa said.

He was blowing up the bladder. It made a little white balloon, and he tied the end tight with a string and gave it to Mary and Laura to play with. They could throw it into the air and spat it back and forth with their hands. Or it would bounce along the ground and they could kick it. But even better fun than a balloon was the pig's tail.

Pa skinned it for them carefully, and into the large end he thrust a sharpened stick. Ma opened the front of the cookstove and raked hot coals out into the iron hearth. Then Laura and Mary took turns holding the pig's tail over the coals.

It sizzled and fried, and drops of fat dripped off it and blazed on the coals. Ma sprinkled it with salt. Their hands and their faces got very hot, and Laura burned her finger, but she was so excited she did not care. Roasting the pig's tail was such fun that it was hard to play fair, taking turns.

At last it was done. It was nicely browned all over, and how good it smelled! They carried it into the yard to cool it, and even before it was cool enough they began tasting it and burned their tongues.

They ate every little bit of meat off the bones, and then they gave the bones to Jack. And that was the end of the pig's tail. There would not be another one till next year.

Uncle Henry went home after dinner, and Pa went away to his work in the Big Woods. But for Laura and Mary and Ma, Butchering Time had only begun. There was a great deal for Ma to do, and Laura and Mary helped her.

All that day and the next, Ma was trying out the lard in big iron pots on the cookstove. Laura and Mary carried wood and watched the fire. It must be hot, but not too hot, or the lard would burn. The big pots simmered and boiled, but they must not smoke. From time to time Ma skimmed out the brown cracklings. She put them in a cloth and squeezed out every bit of the lard, and then she put the cracklings away. She would use them to flavor johnny-cake later.

Cracklings were very good to eat, but Laura and Mary could have only a taste. They were too rich for little girls, Ma said.

Ma scraped and cleaned the head carefully, and then she boiled it till all the meat fell off the bones. She chopped the meat fine with her chopping knife in the wooden bowl, she seasoned it with pepper and salt and spices. Then she mixed the pot-liquor with it, and set it away in a pan to cool. When it was cool it would cut in slices, and that was head-cheese.

The little pieces of meat, lean and fat, that had been cut off the large pieces, Ma chopped and chopped until it was all chopped fine. She seasoned it with salt and pepper and with dried sage leaves from the garden. Then with her hands she tossed and turned it until it was well mixed, and she molded it into balls. She put the balls in a pan out in the shed, where they would freeze and be good to eat all winter. That was the sausage.

When Butchering Time was over, there were the sausages and the headcheese, the big jars of lard and the keg of white salt-pork out in the shed, and in the attic hung the smoked hams and shoulders.

The little house was fairly bursting with good food stored away for the long winter. The pantry and the shed and the cellar were full, and so was the attic.

Laura and Mary must play in the house now, for it was cold outdoors and the brown leaves were all falling from the trees. The fire in the cookstove never went out. At night Pa banked it with ashes to keep the coals alive till morning.

The attic was a lovely place to play. The large, round, colored pumpkins made beautiful chairs and tables. The red peppers and the onions dangled overhead. The hams and the venison hung in their paper wrappings, and all the bunches of dried herbs, the spicy herbs for cooking and the bitter herbs for medicine, gave the place a dusty-spicy smell.

Often the wind howled outside with a cold and lonesome sound. But in the attic Laura and Mary played house with the squashes and the pumpkins, and everything was snug and cosy.

Mary was bigger than Laura, and she had a rag doll named Nettie. Laura had only a corncob wrapped in a handkerchief, but it was a good doll. It was named Susan. It wasn't Susan's fault that she was only a corncob. Sometimes Mary let Laura hold Nettie, but she did it only when Susan couldn't see.

The best times of all were at night. After supper Pa brought his traps in from the shed to grease them by the fire. He rubbed them bright and greased the hinges of the jaws and the springs of the pans with a feather dipped in bear's grease.

There were small traps and middle-sized traps and great bear traps with teeth in their jaws that Pa said would break a man's leg if they shut onto it.

While he greased the traps, Pa told Laura and Mary little jokes and stories, and afterward he would play his fiddle.

The doors and windows were tightly shut, and the cracks of the window frames stuffed with cloth, to keep out the cold. But Black Susan, the cat, came and went as she pleased, day and night, through the swinging door of the cat-hole in the bottom of the front door. She always went very quickly, so the door would not catch her tail when it fell shut behind her.

One night when Pa was greasing the traps he watched Black Susan come in, and he said:

"There was once a man who had two cats, a big cat and a little cat."

Laura and Mary ran to lean on his knees and hear the rest.

"He had two cats," Pa repeated, "a big cat and a little cat. So he made a big cat-hole in his door for the big cat. And then he made a little cat-hole for the little cat."

There Pa stopped.

"But why couldn't the little cat—" Mary began.

"Because the big cat wouldn't let it," Laura interrupted.

"Laura, that is very rude. You must never interrupt," said Pa.

"But I see," he said, "that either one of you has more sense than the man who cut the two cat-holes in his door."

Then he laid away the traps, and he took his fiddle out of its box and began to play. That was the best time of all.

WINTER DAYS AND WINTER NIGHTS

The first snow came, and the bitter cold. Every morning Pa took his gun and his traps and was gone all day in the Big Woods, setting the small traps for muskrats and mink along the creeks, the middle-sized traps for foxes and wolves in the woods. He set out the big bear traps hoping to get a fat bear before they all went into their dens for the winter.

One morning he came back, took the horses and sled, and hurried away again. He had shot a bear. Laura and Mary jumped up and down and clapped their hands, they were so glad. Mary shouted:

"I want the drumstick! I want the drumstick!"

Mary did not know how big a bear's drumstick is.

When Pa came back he had both a bear and a pig in the wagon. He had been going through the woods, with a big bear trap in his hands and the gun on his shoulder, when he walked around a big pine tree covered with snow, and the bear was behind the tree.

The bear had just killed the pig and was picking it up to eat it. Pa said the bear was standing up on its hind legs, holding the pig in its paws just as though they were hands.

Pa shot the bear, and there was no way of knowing where the pig came from nor whose pig it was.

"So I just brought home the bacon," Pa said.

There was plenty of fresh meat to last for a long time. The days and the nights were so cold that the pork in a box and the bear meat hanging in the little shed outside the back door were solidly frozen and did not thaw.

When Ma wanted fresh meat for dinner Pa took the ax and cut off a chunk of frozen bear meat or pork. But the sausage balls, or the salt pork, or the smoked hams and the venison, Ma could get for herself from the shed or the attic.

The snow kept coming till it was drifted and banked against the house. In the mornings the window panes were covered with frost in beautiful pictures of trees and flowers and fairies.

Ma said that Jack Frost came in the night and made the pictures, while everyone was asleep. Laura thought that Jack Frost was a little man all snowy white, wearing a glittering white pointed cap and soft white knee-boots made of deer-skin. His coat was white and his mittens were white, and he did not carry a gun on his back, but in his hands he had shining sharp tools with which he carved the pictures.

Laura and Mary were allowed to take Ma's

thimble and make pretty patterns of circles in the frost on the glass. But they never spoiled the pictures that Jack Frost had made in the night.

When they put their mouths close to the pane and blew their breath on it, the white frost melted and ran in drops down the glass. Then they could see the drifts of snow outdoors and the great trees standing bare and black, making thin blue shadows on the white snow.

Laura and Mary helped Ma with the work. Every morning there were the dishes to wipe. Mary wiped more of them than Laura because she was bigger, but Laura always wiped carefully her own little cup and plate.

By the time the dishes were all wiped and set away, the trundle bed was aired. Then, standing one on each side, Laura and Mary straightened the covers, tucked them in well at the foot and the sides, plumped up the pillows and put them in place. Then Ma pushed the trundle bed into its place under the big bed.

After this was done, Ma began the work that

belonged to that day. Each day had its own proper work. Ma used to say:

"Wash on Monday,
Iron on Tuesday,
Mend on Wednesday,
Churn on Thursday,
Clean on Friday,
Bake on Saturday,
Rest on Sunday."

Laura liked the churning and the baking days best of all the week.

In winter the cream was not yellow as it was in summer, and butter churned from it was white and not so pretty. Ma liked everything on her table to be pretty, so in the wintertime she colored the butter.

After she had put the cream in the tall crockery churn and set it near the stove to warm, she washed and scraped a long orange-colored carrot. Then she grated it on the bottom of the old, leaky tin pan that Pa had punched full of nail-holes for her. Ma rubbed the carrot across the roughness until she had rubbed it all through the holes, and when she lifted up the pan, there was a soft, juicy mound of grated carrot.

She put this in a little pan of milk on the stove and when the milk was hot she poured milk and carrot into a cloth bag. Then she squeezed the bright yellow milk into the churn, where it colored all the cream. Now the butter would be yellow.

Laura and Mary were allowed to eat the carrot after the milk had been squeezed out. Mary thought she ought to have the larger share because she was older, and Laura said she should have it because she was littler. But Ma said they must divide it evenly. It was very good.

When the cream was ready, Ma scalded the long wooden churn-dash, put it in the churn, and dropped the wooden churn-cover over it. The churn-cover had a little round hole in the middle, and Ma moved the dash up and down, up and down, through the hole.

She churned for a long time. Mary could sometimes churn while Ma rested, but the dash was too heavy for Laura.

At first the splashes of cream showed thick and smooth around the little hole. After a long time, they began to look grainy. Then Ma churned more slowly, and on the dash there began to appear tiny grains of yellow butter.

When Ma took off the churn-cover, there was the butter in a golden lump, drowning in the buttermilk. Then Ma took out the lump with a wooden paddle, into a wooden bowl, and she washed it many times in cold water, turning it over and over and working it with the paddle until the water ran clear. After that she salted it.

Now came the best part of the churning. Ma molded the butter. On the loose bottom of the wooden butter-mold was carved the picture of a strawberry with two strawberry leaves.

With the paddle Ma packed butter tightly into the mold until it was full. Then she turned it upside-down over a plate, and pushed on the handle of the loose bottom. The little, firm pat of golden butter came out, with the strawberry and its leaves molded on the top.

Laura and Mary watched, breathless, one on each side of Ma, while the golden little butter-pats, each with its strawberry on the top, dropped onto the plate as Ma put all the butter through the mold. Then Ma gave them each a drink of good, fresh buttermilk.

On Saturdays, when Ma made the bread, they each had a little piece of dough to make into a little loaf. They might have a bit of cookie dough, too, to make little cookies, and once Laura even made a pie in her patty-pan.

After the day's work was done, Ma sometimes cut paper dolls for them. She cut the dolls out of stiff white paper, and drew the faces with a pencil. Then from bits of colored paper she cut dresses and hats, ribbons and laces, so that Laura and Mary could dress their dolls beautifully.

But the best time of all was at night, when Pa came home.

He would come in from his tramping through the snowy woods with tiny icicles hanging on the ends of his mustaches. He would hang his gun on the wall over the door, throw off his fur cap and coat and mittens, and call: "Where's my little half-pint of sweet cider half drunk up?"

That was Laura, because she was so small.

Laura and Mary would run to climb on his knees and sit there while he warmed himself by the fire. Then he would put on his coat and cap and mittens again and go out to do the chores and bring in plenty of wood for the fire.

Sometimes, when Pa had walked his trap-lines quickly because the traps were empty, or when he had got some game sooner than usual, he would come home early. Then he would have time to play with Laura and Mary.

One game they loved was called mad dog. Pa would run his fingers through his thick, brown hair, standing it all up on end. Then he dropped on all fours and, growling, he chased Laura and Mary all around the room, trying to get them cornered where they couldn't get away.

They were quick at dodging and running, but once he caught them against the wood-box, behind the stove. They couldn't get past Pa, and there was no other way out.

Then Pa growled so terribly, his hair was so wild and his eyes so fierce that it all seemed real. Mary was so frightened that she could not move. But as Pa came nearer Laura screamed, and with a wild leap and a scramble she went over the wood-box, dragging Mary with her.

And at once there was no mad dog at all. There was only Pa standing there with his blue eyes shining, looking at Laura.

"Well!" he said to her. "You're only a little half-pint of cider half drunk up, but by Jinks! you're as strong as a little French horse!"

"You shouldn't frighten the children so, Charles," Ma said. "Look how big their eyes are."

Pa looked, and then he took down his fiddle. He began to play and sing.

"*Yankee Doodle went to town,*
He wore his striped trousies,
He swore he couldn't see the town,
There was so many houses."

Laura and Mary forgot all about the mad dog.

"*And there he saw some great big guns,*
Big as a log of maple,
And every time they turned 'em round,
It took two yoke of cattle.

"*And every time they fired 'em off,*
It took a horn of powder,
It made a noise like father's gun,
Only a nation louder."

Pa was keeping time with his foot, and Laura clapped her hands to the music when he sang,

"*And I'll sing Yankee Doodle-de-do,*
And I'll sing Yankee Doodle,
And I'll sing Yankee Doodle-de-do,
And I'll sing Yankee Doodle!"

All alone in the wild Big Woods, and the snow, and the cold, the little log house was warm and snug and cosy. Pa and Ma and Mary and Laura and Baby Carrie were comfortable and happy there, especially at night.

Then the fire was shining on the hearth, the cold and the dark and the wild beasts were all shut out, and Jack the brindle bulldog and Black Susan the cat lay blinking at the flames in the fireplace.

Ma sat in her rocking chair, sewing by the light of the lamp on the table. The lamp was bright and shiny. There was salt in the bottom of its glass bowl with the kerosene, to keep the kerosene from exploding, and there were bits of red flannel among the salt to make it pretty. It was pretty.

Laura loved to look at the lamp, with its glass chimney so clean and sparkling, its yellow flame burning so steadily, and its bowl of clear kerosene colored red by the bits of flannel. She loved to look at the fire in the fireplace, flickering and changing all the time, burning yellow and red and sometimes green above the logs, and hovering blue over the golden and ruby coals.

And then, Pa told stories.

When Laura and Mary begged him for a story, he would take them on his knees and tickle their faces with his long whiskers until they laughed aloud. His eyes were blue and merry.

One night Pa looked at Black Susan, stretching herself before the fire and running her claws out and in, and he said:

"Do you know that a panther is a cat? a great, big, wild cat?"

"No," said Laura.

"Well, it is," said Pa. "Just imagine Black Susan bigger than Jack, and fiercer than Jack when he growls. Then she would be just like a panther."

He settled Laura and Mary more comfortably on his knees and he said, "I'll tell you about Grandpa and the panther."

"Your Grandpa?" Laura asked.

"No, Laura, your Grandpa. My father."

"Oh," Laura said, and she wriggled closer

against Pa's arm. She knew her Grandpa. He lived far away in the Big Woods, in a big log house. Pa began:

THE STORY OF GRANDPA
AND THE PANTHER

"Your Grandpa went to town one day and was late starting home. It was dark when he came riding his horse through the Big Woods, so dark that he could hardly see the road, and when he heard a panther scream he was frightened, for he had no gun."

"How does a panther scream?" Laura asked.

"Like a woman," said Pa. "Like this." Then he screamed so that Laura and Mary shivered with terror.

Ma jumped in her chair, and said, "Mercy, Charles!"

But Laura and Mary loved to be scared like that.

"The horse, with Grandpa on him, ran fast, for it was frightened, too. But it could not get away from the panther. The panther followed through the dark woods. It was a hungry panther, and it came as fast as the horse could run. It screamed now on this side of the road, now on the other side, and it was always close behind.

"Grandpa leaned forward in the saddle and urged the horse to run faster. The horse was running as fast as it could possibly run, and still the panther screamed close behind.

"Then Grandpa caught a glimpse of it, as it leaped from treetop to treetop, almost overhead.

"It was a huge, black panther, leaping through the air like Black Susan leaping on a mouse. It was many, many times bigger than Black Susan. It was so big that if it leaped on Grandpa it could kill him with its enormous, slashing claws and its long sharp teeth.

"Grandpa, on his horse, was running away from it just as a mouse runs from a cat.

"The panther did not scream any more. Grandpa did not see it any more. But he knew that it was coming, leaping after him in the dark woods behind him. The horse ran with all its might.

"At last the horse ran up to Grandpa's house. Grandpa saw the panther springing. Grandpa jumped off the horse, against the door. He burst through the door and slammed it behind him. The panther landed on the horse's back, just where Grandpa had been.

"The horse screamed terribly, and ran. He was running away into the Big Woods, with the panther riding on his back and ripping his back with its claws. But Grandpa grabbed his gun from the wall and got to the window, just in time to shoot the panther dead.

"Grandpa said he would never again go into the Big Woods without his gun."

When Pa told this story, Laura and Mary shivered and snuggled closer to him. They were safe and snug on his knees, with his strong arms around them.

They liked to be there, before the warm fire, with Black Susan purring on the hearth and good dog Jack stretched out beside her. When they heard a wolf howl, Jack's head lifted and the hairs rose stiff along his back.

But Laura and Mary listened to that lonely sound in the dark and the cold of the Big Woods, and they were not afraid.

They were cosy and comfortable in their little house made of logs, with the snow drifted around it and the wind crying because it could not get in by the fire.

THE LONG RIFLE

Every evening before he began to tell stories, Pa made the bullets for his next day's hunting.

Laura and Mary helped him. They brought the big, long-handled spoon, and the box full of bits of lead, and the bullet-mold. Then while he squatted on the hearth and made the bullets, they sat one on each side of him, and watched.

First he melted the bits of lead in the big spoon held in the coals. When the lead was melted, he poured it carefully from the spoon into the little hole in the bullet-mold. He waited a minute, then he opened the mold, and out dropped a bright new bullet onto the hearth.

The bullet was too hot to touch, but it shone so temptingly that sometimes Laura or Mary could not help touching it. Then they burned their fingers. But they did not say anything, because Pa had told them never to touch a new bullet. If they burned their fingers, that was their own fault; they should have minded him. So they put their fingers in their mouths to cool them, and watched Pa make more bullets.

There would be a shining pile of them on the hearth before Pa stopped. He let them cool, then with his jack-knife he trimmed off the little lumps left by the hole in the mold. He gathered up the tiny shavings of lead and saved them carefully, to melt again the next time he made bullets.

The finished bullets he put into his bullet pouch. This was a little bag which Ma had made beautifully of buckskin, from a buck Pa had shot.

After the bullets were made, Pa would take his gun down from the wall and clean it. Out in the snowy woods all day, it might have gathered a little dampness, and the inside of the barrel was sure to be dirty from powder smoke.

So Pa would take the ramrod from its place under the gun barrel, and fasten a piece of clean cloth on its end. He stood the butt of the gun in a pan on the hearth and poured boiling water from the tea kettle into the gun barrel. Then quickly he dropped the ramrod in and rubbed it up and down, up and down, while the hot water blackened with powder smoke spurted out through the little hole on which the cap was placed when the gun was loaded.

Pa kept pouring in more water and washing the gun barrel with the cloth on the ramrod until the water ran out clear. Then the gun was clean. The water must always be boiling, so that the heated steel would dry instantly.

Then Pa put a clean, greased rag on the

ramrod, and while the gun barrel was still hot he greased it well on the inside. With another clean, greased cloth he rubbed it all over, outside, until every bit of it was oiled and sleek. After that he rubbed and polished the gunstock until the wood of it was bright and shining, too.

Now he was ready to load the gun again, and Laura and Mary must help him. Standing straight and tall, holding the long gun upright on its butt, while Laura and Mary stood on either side of him, Pa said:

"You watch me, now, and tell me if I make a mistake."

So they watched very carefully, but he never made a mistake.

Laura handed him the smooth, polished cowhorn full of gunpowder. The top of the horn was a little metal cap. Pa filled this cap full of the gunpowder and poured the powder down the barrel of the gun. Then he shook the gun a little, and tapped the barrel, to be sure that all the powder was together in the bottom.

"Where's my patch box?" he asked then, and

Mary gave him the little tin box full of little pieces of greased cloth. Pa laid one of these bits of greasy cloth over the muzzle of the gun, put one of the shiny new bullets on it, and with the ramrod he pushed the bullet and the cloth down the gun barrel.

Then he pounded them tightly against the powder. When he hit them with the ramrod, the ramrod bounced up in the gun barrel, and Pa caught it and thrust it down again. He did this for a long time.

Next he put the ramrod back in its place against the gun barrel. Then taking a box of caps from his pocket, he raised the hammer of the gun and slipped one of the little bright caps over the hollow pin that was under the hammer.

He let the hammer down, slowly and carefully. If it came down quickly—bang!—the gun would go off.

Now the gun was loaded, and Pa laid it on its hooks over the door.

When Pa was at home the gun always lay across those two wooden hooks above the door.

Pa had whittled the hooks out of a green stick with his knife, and had driven their straight ends deep into holes in the log. The hooked ends curved upward and held the gun securely.

The gun was always loaded, and always above the door so that Pa could get it quickly and easily, any time he needed a gun.

When Pa went into the Big Woods, he always made sure that the bullet pouch was full of bullets, and that the tin patch box and the box of caps were with it in his pockets. The powder horn and a small sharp hatchet hung at his belt and he carried the gun ready loaded on his shoulder.

He always reloaded the gun as soon as he had fired it, for, he said, he did not want to meet trouble with an empty gun.

Whenever he shot at a wild animal, he had to stop and load the gun—measure the powder, put it in and shake it down, put in the patch and the bullet and pound them down, and then put a fresh cap under the hammer—before he could shoot again. When he shot at a bear or a panther, he must kill it with the first shot.

A wounded bear or panther could kill a man before he had time to load his gun again.

But Laura and Mary were never afraid when Pa went alone into the Big Woods. They knew he could always kill bears and panthers with the first shot.

After the bullets were made and the gun was loaded, came story-telling time.

"Tell us about the Voice in the Woods," Laura would beg him.

Pa crinkled up his eyes at her. "Oh, no!" he said. "You don't want to hear about the time I was a naughty little boy."

"Oh, yes, we do! We do!" Laura and Mary said. So Pa began.

THE STORY OF PA AND THE VOICE IN THE WOODS

"When I was a little boy, not much bigger than Mary, I had to go every afternoon to find the cows in the woods and drive them home. My father told me never to play by the way, but to hurry and bring the cows home before dark, because there were bears and wolves and panthers in the woods.

"One day I started earlier than usual, so I thought I did not need to hurry. There were so many things to see in the woods that I forgot that dark was coming. There were red squirrels in the trees, chipmunks scurrying through the leaves, and little rabbits playing games together in the open places. Little rabbits, you know, always have games together before they go to bed.

"I began to play I was a mighty hunter, stalking the wild animals and the Indians. I played I was fighting the Indians, until the woods seemed full of wild men, and then all at once I heard the birds twittering 'good night.' It was dusky in the path, and dark in the woods.

"I knew that I must get the cows home quickly, or it would be black night before they were safe in the barn. And I couldn't find the cows!

"I listened, but I could not hear their bells. I called, but the cows didn't come.

"I was afraid of the dark and the wild beasts,

but I dared not go home to my father without the cows. So I ran through the woods, hunting and calling. All the time the shadows were getting thicker and darker, and the woods seemed larger, and the trees and the bushes looked strange.

"I could not find the cows anywhere. I climbed up hills, looking for them and calling, and I went down into dark ravines, calling and looking. I stopped and listened for the cow-bells and there was not a sound but the rustling of leaves.

"Then I heard loud breathing and thought a panther was there, in the dark behind me. But it was only my own breathing.

"My bare legs were scratched by the briars, and when I ran through the bushes their branches struck me. But I kept on, looking and calling, 'Sukey! Sukey!'

"'Sukey! Sukey!' I shouted with all my might. 'Sukey!'

"Right over my head something asked, 'Who?'

"My hair stood straight on end.

"'Who? Who?' the Voice said again. And then *how* I did run!

"I forgot all about the cows. All I wanted was to get out of the dark woods, to get home.

"That thing in the dark came after me and called again, 'Who-oo?'

"I ran with all my might. I ran till I couldn't breathe and still I kept on running. Something grabbed my foot, and down I went. Up I jumped, and then I *ran*. Not even a wolf could have caught me.

"At last I came out of the dark woods, by the barn. There stood all the cows, waiting to be let through the bars. I let them in, and then ran to the house.

"My father looked up and said, 'Young man, what makes you so late? Been playing by the way?'

"I looked down at my feet, and then I saw that one big-toe nail had been torn clean off. I had been so scared that I had not felt it hurt until that minute."

Pa always stopped telling the story here, and waited until Laura said:

"Go on, Pa! Please go on."

"Well," Pa said, "then your Grandpa went out into the yard and cut a stout switch. And he came back into the house and gave me a good thrashing, so that I would remember to mind him after that.

"'A big boy nine years old is old enough to remember to mind,' he said. 'There's a good reason for what I tell you to do,' he said, 'and if you'll do as you're told, no harm will come to you.'"

"Yes, yes, Pa!" Laura would say, bouncing up and down on Pa's knee. "And then what did he say?"

"He said, 'If you'd obeyed me, as you should, you wouldn't have been out in the Big Woods after dark, and you wouldn't have been scared by a screech-owl.'"

CHRISTMAS

Christmas was coming.

The little log house was almost buried in snow. Great drifts were banked against the walls and windows, and in the morning when Pa opened the door, there was a wall of snow as high as Laura's head. Pa took the shovel and shoveled it away, and then he shoveled a path to the barn, where the horses and the cows were snug and warm in their stalls.

The days were clear and bright. Laura and Mary stood on chairs by the window and looked out across the glittering snow at the glittering trees. Snow was piled all along their bare, dark branches, and it sparkled in the sunshine. Icicles hung from the eaves of the house to the snowbanks, great icicles as large at the top as Laura's arm. They were like glass and full of sharp lights.

Pa's breath hung in the air like smoke, when he came along the path from the barn. He breathed it out in clouds and it froze in white frost on his mustache and beard.

When he came in, stamping the snow from his boots, and caught Laura up in a bear's hug against his cold, big coat, his mustache was beaded with little drops of melting frost.

Every night he was busy, working on a large piece of board and two small pieces. He whittled them with his knife, he rubbed them with sandpaper and with the palm of his hand, until when Laura touched them they felt soft and smooth as silk.

Then with his sharp jack-knife he worked at them, cutting the edges of the large one into little peaks and towers, with a large star carved on the very tallest point. He cut little holes through the wood. He cut the holes in shapes of windows, and little stars, and crescent moons, and circles. All around them he carved tiny leaves, and flowers, and birds.

One of the little boards he shaped in a lovely curve, and around its edges he carved leaves and flowers and stars, and through it he cut crescent moons and curlicues.

Around the edges of the smallest board he carved a tiny flowering vine.

He made the tiniest shavings, cutting very slowly and carefully, making whatever he thought would be pretty.

At last he had the pieces finished and one night he fitted them together. When this was done, the large piece was a beautifully carved back for a smooth little shelf across its middle. The large star was at the very top of it. The curved piece supported the shelf underneath, and it was carved beautifully, too. And the little vine ran around the edge of the shelf.

Pa had made this bracket for a Christmas present for Ma. He hung it carefully against the log wall between the windows, and Ma stood her little china woman on the shelf.

The little china woman had a china bonnet on her head, and china curls hung against her china neck. Her china dress was laced across in front, and she wore a pale pink china apron and little gilt china shoes. She was beautiful, standing on the shelf with flowers and leaves and birds and moons carved all around her, and the large star at the very top.

Ma was busy all day long, cooking good things for Christmas. She baked salt-rising bread and rye'n'Injun bread, and Swedish crackers, and a huge pan of baked beans, with salt pork and molasses. She baked vinegar pies and dried-apple pies, and filled a big jar with cookies, and she let Laura and Mary lick the cake spoon.

One morning she boiled molasses and sugar together until they made a thick syrup, and Pa brought in two pans of clean, white snow from outdoors. Laura and Mary each had a pan, and Pa and Ma showed them how to pour the dark syrup in little streams onto the snow.

They made circles, and curlicues, and squiggledy things, and these hardened at once and were candy. Laura and Mary might eat one piece each, but the rest was saved for Christmas Day.

All this was done because Aunt Eliza and Uncle Peter and the cousins, Peter and Alice and Ella, were coming to spend Christmas.

The day before Christmas they came. Laura and Mary heard the gay ringing of sleigh bells, growing louder every moment, and then the big bobsled came out of the woods and drove up to the gate. Aunt Eliza and Uncle Peter and the cousins were in it, all covered up, under blankets and robes and buffalo skins.

They were wrapped up in so many coats and mufflers and veils and shawls that they looked like big, shapeless bundles.

When they all came in, the little house was full and running over. Black Susan ran out and hid in the barn, but Jack leaped in circles through the snow, barking as though he would never stop. Now there were cousins to play with!

As soon as Aunt Eliza had unwrapped them, Peter and Alice and Ella and Laura and Mary began to run and shout. At last Aunt Eliza told them to be quiet. Then Alice said:

"I'll tell you what let's do. Let's make pictures."

Alice said they must go outdoors to do it, and Ma thought it was too cold for Laura to play outdoors. But when she saw how disappointed Laura was, she said she might go, after all, for a little while. She put on Laura's coat and mittens and the warm cape with the hood, and wrapped a muffler around her neck, and let her go.

Laura had never had so much fun. All morning she played outdoors in the snow with Alice and Ella and Peter and Mary, making pictures. The way they did it was this:

Each one by herself climbed up on a stump, and then all at once, holding their arms out wide, they fell off the stumps into the soft, deep snow. They fell flat on their faces. Then they tried to get up without spoiling the marks they made when they fell. If they did it well, there in the snow were five holes, shaped almost exactly like four little girls and a boy, arms and legs and all. They called these their pictures.

They played so hard all day that when night came they were too excited to sleep. But they must sleep, or Santa Claus would not come. So they hung their stockings by the fireplace, and said their prayers, and went to bed—Alice and Ella and Mary and Laura all in one big bed on the floor.

Peter had the trundle bed. Aunt Eliza and Uncle Peter were going to sleep in the big bed, and another bed was made on the attic floor for Pa and Ma. The buffalo robes and all the blankets had been brought in from Uncle Peter's sled, so there were enough covers for everybody.

Pa and Ma and Aunt Eliza and Uncle Peter sat by the fire, talking. And just as Laura was drifting off to sleep, she heard Uncle Peter say:

"Eliza had a narrow squeak the other day, when I was away at Lake City. You know Prince, that big dog of mine?"

Laura was wide awake at once. She always liked to hear about dogs. She lay still as a mouse, and looked at the fire-light flickering on the log walls, and listened to Uncle Peter.

"Well," Uncle Peter said, "early in the morning Eliza started to the spring to get a pail of water, and Prince was following her. She got to the edge of the ravine, where the path goes down to the spring, and all of a sudden Prince set his teeth in the back of her skirt and pulled.

"You know what a big dog he is. Eliza scolded him, but he wouldn't let go, and he's so big and strong she couldn't get away from him. He kept backing and pulling, till he tore a piece out of her skirt."

"It was my blue print," Aunt Eliza said to Ma.

"Dear me!" Ma said.

"He tore a big piece right out of the back of it," Aunt Eliza said. "I was so mad I could have whipped him for it. But he growled at me."

"Prince growled at you?" Pa said.

"Yes," said Aunt Eliza.

"So then she started on again toward the spring," Uncle Peter went on. "But Prince jumped into the path ahead of her and snarled at her. He paid no attention to her talking and scolding. He just kept on showing his teeth and snarling, and when she tried to get past him he kept in front of her and snapped at her. That scared her."

"I should think it would!" Ma said.

"He was so savage, I thought he was going to bite me," said Aunt Eliza. "I believe he would have."

"I never heard of such a thing!" said Ma. "What on earth did you do?"

"I turned right around and ran into the house where the children were, and slammed the door," Aunt Eliza answered.

"Of course Prince was savage with strangers," said Uncle Peter. "But he was always so kind to Eliza and the children I felt perfectly safe to leave them with him. Eliza couldn't understand it at all.

"After she got into the house he kept pacing around it and growling. Every time she started to open the door he jumped at her and snarled."

"Had he gone mad?" said Ma.

"That's what I thought," Aunt Eliza said. "I didn't know what to do. There I was, shut up in the house with the children, and not daring to go out. And we didn't have any water. I couldn't even get any snow to melt. Every time I opened the door so much as a crack, Prince acted like he would tear me to pieces."

"How long did this go on?" Pa asked.

"All day, till late in the afternoon," Aunt Eliza said. "Peter had taken the gun, or I would have shot him."

"Along late in the afternoon," Uncle Peter said, "he got quiet, and lay down in front of the door. Eliza thought he was asleep, and she made up her mind to try to slip past him and get to the spring for some water.

"So she opened the door very quietly, but of course he woke up right away. When he saw she had the water pail in her hand, he got up and walked ahead of her to the spring, just the same as usual. And there, all around the spring in the snow, were the fresh tracks of a panther."

"The tracks were as big as my hand," said Aunt Eliza.

"Yes," Uncle Peter said, "he was a big fellow. His tracks were the biggest I ever saw. He would have got Eliza sure, if Prince had let her go to the spring in the morning. I saw the tracks. He had been lying up in that big oak over the spring, waiting for some animal to come there for water. Undoubtedly he would have dropped down on her.

"Night was coming on, when she saw the tracks, and she didn't waste any time getting back to the house with her pail of water. Prince followed close behind her, looking back into the ravine now and then."

"I took him into the house with me," Aunt Eliza said, "and we all stayed inside, till Peter came home."

"Did you get him?" Pa asked Uncle Peter.

"No," Uncle Peter said. "I took my gun and hunted all round the place, but I couldn't find him. I saw some more of his tracks. He'd gone on north, farther into the Big Woods."

Alice and Ella and Mary were all wide awake now, and Laura put her head under the covers and whispered to Alice, "My! weren't you scared?"

Alice whispered back that she was scared, but Ella was scareder. And Ella whispered that she wasn't, either, any such thing.

"Well, anyway, you made more fuss about being thirsty," Alice whispered.

They lay there whispering about it till Ma said: "Charles, those children never will get to sleep unless you play for them." So Pa got his fiddle.

The room was still and warm and full of fire-light. Ma's shadow, and Aunt Eliza's and Uncle Peter's were big and quivering on the walls in the flickering fire-light, and Pa's fiddle sang merrily to itself.

It sang "Money Musk," and "The Red Heifer," "The Devil's Dream," and "Arkansas Traveler." And Laura went to sleep while Pa and the fiddle were both softly singing:

"My darling Nelly Gray, they have taken you away,
And I'll never see my darling any more. . . ."

In the morning they all woke up almost at the same moment. They looked at their stockings, and something was in them. Santa Claus had been there. Alice and Ella and Laura in their red flannel nightgowns, and Peter in his red flannel nightshirt, all ran shouting to see what he had brought.

In each stocking there was a pair of bright red mittens, and there was a long, flat stick of red-and-white-striped peppermint candy, all beautifully notched along each side.

They were all so happy they could hardly speak at first. They just looked with shining eyes at those lovely Christmas presents. But Laura was happiest of all. Laura had a rag doll.

She was a beautiful doll. She had a face of white cloth with black button eyes. A black pencil had made her eyebrows, and her cheeks and her mouth were red with the ink made from pokeberries. Her hair was black yarn that had been knit and raveled, so that it was curly.

She had little red flannel stockings and little black cloth gaiters for shoes, and her dress was pretty pink and blue calico.

She was so beautiful that Laura could not say a word. She just held her tight and forgot everything else. She did not know that everyone was looking at her, till Aunt Eliza said:

"Did you ever see such big eyes!"

The other girls were not jealous because Laura had mittens, and candy, *and* a doll, because Laura was the littlest girl, except Baby Carrie and Aunt Eliza's little baby, Dolly Varden. The babies were too small for dolls. They were so small they did not even know about Santa Claus. They just put their fingers in their mouths and wriggled because of all the excitement.

Laura sat down on the edge of the bed and held her doll. She loved her red mittens and she loved the candy, but she loved her doll best of all. She named her Charlotte.

Then they all looked at each other's mittens, and tried on their own, and Peter bit a large piece out of his stick of candy, but Alice and Ella and Mary and Laura licked theirs, to make it last longer.

"Well, well!" Uncle Peter said. "Isn't there even one stocking with nothing but a switch in it? My, my, have you all been such good children?"

But they didn't believe that Santa Claus could, really, have given any of them nothing but a switch. That happened to some children, but it couldn't happen to them. It was so hard to be good all the time, every day, for a whole year.

"You mustn't tease the children, Peter," Aunt Eliza said.

Ma said, "Laura, aren't you going to let the other girls hold your doll?" She meant, "Little girls must not be so selfish."

So Laura let Mary take the beautiful doll, and then Alice held her a minute, and then Ella. They smoothed the pretty dress and admired the red flannel stockings and the gaiters, and the curly woolen hair. But Laura was glad when at last Charlotte was safe in her arms again.

Pa and Uncle Peter had each a pair of new, warm mittens, knit in little squares of red and white. Ma and Aunt Eliza had made them.

Aunt Eliza had brought Ma a large red apple stuck full of cloves. How good it smelled! And it would not spoil, for so many cloves would keep it sound and sweet.

Ma gave Aunt Eliza a little needle-book she had made, with bits of silk for covers and soft white flannel leaves into which to stick the needles. The flannel would keep the needles from rusting.

They all admired Ma's beautiful bracket, and Aunt Eliza said that Uncle Peter had made one for her—of course, with different carving.

Santa Claus had not given them anything at all. Santa Claus did not give grown people presents, but that was not because they had not been good. Pa and Ma were good. It was because they were grown up, and grown people must give each other presents.

Then all the presents must be laid away for a little while. Peter went out with Pa and Uncle Peter to do the chores, and Alice and Ella helped Aunt Eliza make the beds, and Laura and Mary set the table, while Ma got breakfast.

For breakfast there were pancakes, and Ma made a pancake man for each one of the children. Ma called each one in turn to bring her plate, and each could stand by the stove and watch, while with the spoonful of batter Ma put on the arms and the legs and the head. It was exciting to watch her turn the whole little man over, quickly and carefully, on a hot griddle. When it was done, she put it smoking hot on the plate.

Peter ate the head off his man, right away. But Alice and Ella and Mary and Laura ate theirs slowly in little bits, first the arms and legs and then the middle, saving the head for the last.

Today the weather was so cold that they could not play outdoors, but there were the new mittens to admire, and the candy to lick. And they all sat on the floor together and looked at the pictures in the Bible, and the pictures of all kinds of animals and birds in Pa's big green book. Laura kept Charlotte in her arms the whole time.

Then there was the Christmas dinner. Alice and Ella and Peter and Mary and Laura did not say a word at table, for they knew that children should be seen and not heard. But they did not need to ask for second helpings. Ma and Aunt

Eliza kept their plates full and let them eat all the good things they could hold.

"Christmas comes but once a year," said Aunt Eliza.

Dinner was early, because Aunt Eliza, Uncle Peter and the cousins had such a long way to go.

"Best the horses can do," Uncle Peter said, "we'll hardly make it home before dark."

So as soon as they had eaten dinner, Uncle Peter and Pa went to put the horses to the sled, while Ma and Aunt Eliza wrapped up the cousins.

They pulled heavy woolen stockings over the woolen stockings and the shoes they were already wearing. They put on mittens and coats and warm hoods and shawls, and wrapped mufflers around their necks and thick woolen veils over their faces. Ma slipped piping hot baked potatoes into their pockets to keep their fingers warm, and Aunt Eliza's flatirons were hot on the stove, ready to put at their feet in the sled. The blankets and the quilts and the buffalo robes were warmed, too.

So they all got into the big bobsled, cosy and warm, and Pa tucked the last robe well in around them.

"Good-by! Good-by!" they called, and off they went, the horses trotting gaily and the sleigh bells ringing.

In just a little while the merry sound of the bells was gone, and Christmas was over. But what a happy Christmas it had been!

SUNDAYS

Now the winter seemed long. Laura and Mary began to be tired of staying always in the house. Especially on Sundays, the time went so slowly.

Every Sunday Mary and Laura were dressed from the skin out in their best clothes, with fresh ribbons in their hair. They were very clean, because they had their baths on Saturday night.

In the summer they were bathed in water from the spring. But in the wintertime Pa filled and heaped the washtub with clean snow, and on the cookstove it melted to water. Then close by the warm stove, behind a screen made of a blanket over two chairs, Ma bathed Laura, and then she bathed Mary.

Laura was bathed first, because she was littler than Mary. She had to go to bed early on Saturday nights, with Charlotte, because after she was bathed and put into her clean nightgown, Pa must empty the washtub and fill it with snow again for Mary's bath. Then after Mary came to bed, Ma had her bath behind the blanket, and then Pa had his. And they were all clean, for Sunday.

On Sundays Mary and Laura must not run or shout or be noisy in their play. Mary could not sew on her nine-patch quilt, and Laura could not knit on the tiny mittens she was making for Baby Carrie. They might look quietly at their paper dolls, but they must not make anything new for them. They were not allowed to sew on doll clothes, not even with pins.

They must sit quietly and listen while Ma read Bible stories to them, or stories about lions and tigers and white bears from Pa's big green book, *The Wonders of the Animal World*. They might look at pictures, and they might hold their rag dolls nicely and talk to them. But there was nothing else they could do.

Laura liked best to look at the pictures in the big Bible, with its paper covers. Best of all was the picture of Adam naming the animals.

Adam sat on a rock, and all the animals and birds, big and little, were gathered around him anxiously waiting to be told what kind of animals they were. Adam looked so comfortable. He did not have to be careful to keep his clothes clean, because he had no clothes on. He wore only a skin around his middle.

"Did Adam have good clothes to wear on Sundays?" Laura asked Ma.

"No," Ma said. "Poor Adam, all he had to wear was skins."

Laura did not pity Adam. She wished she had nothing to wear but skins.

One Sunday after supper she could not bear it any longer. She began to play with Jack, and in a few minutes she was running and shouting. Pa told her to sit in her chair and be quiet, but when Laura sat down she began to cry and kick the chair with her heels.

"I hate Sunday!" she said.

Pa put down his book. "Laura," he said sternly, "come here."

Her feet dragged as she went, because she knew she deserved a spanking. But when she reached Pa, he looked at her sorrowfully for a moment, and then took her on his knee and cuddled her against him. He held out his other arm to Mary, and said:

"I'm going to tell you a story about when Grandpa was a boy."

THE STORY OF GRANDPA'S SLED AND THE PIG

"When your Grandpa was a boy, Laura, Sunday did not begin on Sunday morning, as it does now. It began at sundown on Saturday night. Then everyone stopped every kind of work or play.

"Supper was solemn. After supper, Grandpa's father read aloud a chapter of the Bible, while everyone sat straight and still in his chair. Then they all knelt down, and their father said a long prayer. When he said, 'Amen,' they got up from their knees and each took a candle and went to bed. They must go straight to bed, with no playing, laughing, or even talking.

"Sunday morning they ate a cold breakfast, because nothing could be cooked on Sunday. Then they all dressed in their best clothes and walked to church. They walked, because hitching up the horses was work, and no work could be done on Sunday.

"They must walk slowly and solemnly, looking straight ahead. They must not joke or laugh, or even smile. Grandpa and his two brothers walked ahead, and their father and mother walked behind them.

"In church, Grandpa and his brothers must sit perfectly still for two long hours and listen to the sermon. They dared not fidget on the hard bench. They dared not swing their feet.

They dared not turn their heads to look at the windows or the walls or the ceiling of the church. They must sit perfectly motionless, and never for one instant take their eyes from the preacher.

"When church was over, they walked slowly home. They might talk on the way, but they must not talk loudly and they must never laugh or smile. At home they ate a cold dinner which had been cooked the day before. Then all the long afternoon they must sit in a row on a bench and study their catechism, until at last the sun went down and Sunday was over.

"Now Grandpa's home was about halfway down the side of a steep hill. The road went from the top of the hill to the bottom, right past the front door, and in winter it was the best place for sliding downhill that you can possibly imagine.

"One week Grandpa and his two brothers, James and George, were making a new sled. They worked at it every minute of their play-time. It was the best sled they had ever made, and it was so long that all three of them could sit on it, one behind the other. They planned to finish it in time to slide downhill Saturday afternoon. For every Saturday afternoon they had two or three hours to play.

"But that week their father was cutting down trees in the Big Woods. He was working hard and he kept the boys working with him. They did all the morning chores by lantern-light and were hard at work in the woods when the sun came up. They worked till dark, and then there were the chores to do, and after supper they had to go to bed so they could get up early in the morning.

"They had no time to work on the sled until Saturday afternoon. Then they worked at it just as fast as they could, but they didn't get it finished till just as the sun went down, Saturday night.

"After the sun went down, they could not slide downhill, not even once. That would be breaking the Sabbath. So they put the sled in the shed behind the house, to wait until Sunday was over.

"All the two long hours in church next day,

while they kept their feet still and their eyes on the preacher, they were thinking about the sled. At home while they ate dinner they couldn't think of anything else. After dinner their father sat down to read the Bible, and Grandpa and James and George sat as still as mice on their bench with their catechism. But they were thinking about the sled.

"The sun shone brightly and the snow was smooth and glittering on the road; they could see it through the window. It was a perfect day for sliding downhill. They looked at their catechism and they thought about the new sled, and it seemed that Sunday would never end.

"After a long time they heard a snore. They looked at their father, and they saw that his head had fallen against the back of his chair and he was fast asleep.

"Then James looked at George, and James got up from the bench and tiptoed out of the room through the back door. George looked at Grandpa, and George tiptoed after James. And Grandpa looked fearfully at their father, but on tiptoe he followed George and left their father snoring.

"They took their new sled and went quietly up to the top of the hill. They meant to slide down, just once. Then they would put the sled away, and slip back to their bench and the catechism before their father woke up.

"James sat in front on the sled, then George, and then Grandpa, because he was the littlest. The sled started, at first slowly, then faster and faster. It was running, flying, down the long steep hill, but the boys dared not shout. They must slide silently past the house, without waking their father.

"There was no sound except the little whirr of the runners on the snow, and the wind rushing past.

"Then just as the sled was swooping toward the house, a big black pig stepped out of the woods. He walked into the middle of the road and stood there.

"The sled was going so fast it couldn't be stopped. There wasn't time to turn it. The sled went right under the hog and picked him up.

With a squeal he sat down on James, and he kept on squealing, long and loud and shrill, 'Squee-ee-ee-ee-ee! Squee-ee-ee-ee-ee-ee!'

"They flashed by the house, the pig sitting in front, then James, then George, then Grandpa, and they saw their father standing in the doorway looking at them. They couldn't stop, they couldn't hide, there was no time to say anything. Down the hill they went, the hog sitting on James and squealing all the way.

"At the bottom of the hill they stopped. The hog jumped off James and ran away into the woods, still squealing.

"The boys walked slowly and solemnly up the hill. They put the sled away. They sneaked into the house and slipped quietly to their places on the bench. Their father was reading his Bible. He looked up at them without saying a word.

"Then he went on reading, and they studied their catechism.

"But when the sun went down and the Sabbath day was over, their father took them out to the woodshed and tanned their jackets, first James, then George, then Grandpa.

"So you see, Laura and Mary," Pa said, "you may find it hard to be good, but you should be glad that it isn't as hard to be good now as it was when Grandpa was a boy."

"Did little girls have to be as good as that?" Laura asked, and Ma said:

"It was harder for little girls. Because they had to behave like little ladies all the time, not only on Sundays. Little girls could never slide downhill, like boys. Little girls had to sit in the house and stitch on samplers."

"Now run along and let Ma put you to bed," said Pa, and he took his fiddle out of its box.

Laura and Mary lay in their trundle bed and listened to the Sunday hymns, for even the fiddle must not sing the weekday songs on Sundays.

"'Rock of Ages, cleft for me,'" Pa sang, with the fiddle. Then he sang:

> *"Shall I be carried to the skies,*
> *On flowery beds of ease,*
> *While others fought to win the prize,*
> *And sailed through bloody seas?"*

Laura began to float away on the music, and then she heard a clattering noise, and there was Ma by the stove, getting breakfast. It was Monday morning, and Sunday would not come again for a whole week.

That morning when Pa came in to breakfast he caught Laura and said he must give her a spanking.

First he explained that today was her birthday, and she would not grow properly next year unless she had a spanking. And then he spanked so gently and carefully that it did not hurt a bit.

"One—two—three—four—five—six," he counted and spanked, slowly. One spank for each year, and at the last one big spank to grow on.

Then Pa gave her a little wooden man he had whittled out of a stick, to be company for Charlotte. Ma gave her five little cakes, one for each year that Laura had lived with her and Pa. And Mary gave her a new dress for Charlotte. Mary had made the dress herself, when Laura thought she was sewing on her patchwork quilt.

And that night, for a special birthday treat, Pa played "Pop Goes the Weasel" for her.

He sat with Laura and Mary close against his knees while he played. "Now watch," he said. "Watch, and maybe you can see the weasel pop out this time." Then he sang:

> *"A penny for a spool of thread,*
> *Another for a needle,*
> *That's the way the money goes—"*

Laura and Mary bent close, watching, for they knew now was the time.

> *"Pop! (said Pa's finger on the string)*
> *Goes the weasel! (sang the fiddle, plain as*
> *plain.)"*

But Laura and Mary hadn't seen Pa's finger make the string pop.

"Oh, please, please, do it again!" they begged

him. Pa's blue eyes laughed, and the fiddle
went on while he sang:

> "All around the cobbler's bench,
> The monkey chased the weasel,
> The preacher kissed the cobbler's wife—
> Pop! goes the weasel!"

They hadn't seen Pa's finger that time, either.
He was so quick they could never catch him.

So they went laughing to bed and lay listening to Pa and the fiddle singing:

> "There was an old darkey
> And his name was Uncle Ned,
> And he died long ago, long ago.
> There was no wool on the top of his head,
> In the place where the wool ought to grow.

> "His fingers were as long,
> As the cane in the brake,
> His eyes they could hardly see,
> And he had no teeth for to eat the hoe-cake,
> So he had to let the hoe-cake be.

"So hang up the shovel and the hoe,
Lay down the fiddle and the bow,
There's no more work for old Uncle Ned,
For he's gone where the good darkeys go."

Two Big Bears

Then one day Pa said that spring was coming.

In the Big Woods the snow was beginning to thaw. Bits of it dropped from the branches of the trees and made little holes in the softening snowbanks below. At noon all the big icicles along the eaves of the little house quivered and sparkled in the sunshine, and drops of water hung trembling at their tips.

Pa said he must go to town to trade the furs of the wild animals he had been trapping all

winter. So one evening he made a big bundle
of them. There were so many furs that when
they were packed tightly and tied together they
made a bundle almost as big as Pa.

Very early one morning Pa strapped the
bundle of furs on his shoulders, and started to
walk to town. There were so many furs to carry
that he could not take his gun.

Ma was worried, but Pa said that by starting
before sun-up and walking very fast all day he
could get home again before dark.

The nearest town was far away. Laura and
Mary had never seen a town. They had never
seen a store. They had never seen even two
houses standing together. But they knew that
in a town there were many houses, and a store
full of candy and calico and other wonderful
things—powder, and shot, and salt, and store
sugar.

They knew that Pa would trade his furs to
the storekeeper for beautiful things from town,
and all day they were expecting the presents he
would bring them. When the sun sank low

above the treetops and no more drops fell from the tips of the icicles they began to watch eagerly for Pa.

The sun sank out of sight, the woods grew dark, and he did not come. Ma started supper and set the table, but he did not come. It was time to do the chores, and still he had not come.

Ma said that Laura might come with her while she milked the cow. Laura could carry the lantern.

So Laura put on her coat and Ma buttoned it up. And Laura put her hands into her red mittens that hung by a red yarn string around her neck, while Ma lighted the candle in the lantern.

Laura was proud to be helping Ma with the milking, and she carried the lantern very carefully. Its sides were of tin, with places cut in them for the candle-light to shine through.

When Laura walked behind Ma on the path to the barn, the little bits of candle-light from the lantern leaped all around her on the snow. The night was not yet quite dark. The woods were dark, but there was a gray light on the snowy path, and in the sky there were a few faint stars. The stars did not look as warm and bright as the little lights that came from the lantern.

Laura was surprised to see the dark shape of Sukey, the brown cow, standing at the barnyard gate. Ma was surprised, too.

It was too early in the spring for Sukey to be let out in the Big Woods to eat grass. She lived in the barn. But sometimes on warm days Pa left the door of her stall open so she could come into the barnyard. Now Ma and Laura saw her behind the bars, waiting for them.

Ma went up to the gate, and pushed against it to open it. But it did not open very far, because there was Sukey, standing against it. Ma said:

"Sukey, get over!" She reached across the gate and slapped Sukey's shoulder.

Just then one of the dancing little bits of light from the lantern jumped between the bars of the gate, and Laura saw long, shaggy, black fur, and two little, glittering eyes.

Sukey had thin, short, brown fur. Sukey had large, gentle eyes.

Ma said, "Laura, walk back to the house."

So Laura turned around and began to walk toward the house. Ma came behind her. When they had gone part way, Ma snatched her up, lantern and all, and ran. Ma ran with her into the house, and slammed the door.

Then Laura said, "Ma, was it a bear?"

"Yes, Laura," Ma said. "It was a bear."

Laura began to cry. She hung on to Ma and sobbed, "Oh, will he eat Sukey?"

"No," Ma said, hugging her. "Sukey is safe in the barn. Think, Laura—all those big, heavy logs in the barn walls. And the door is heavy and solid, made to keep bears out. No, the bear cannot get in and eat Sukey."

Laura felt better then. "But he could have hurt us, couldn't he?" she asked.

"He didn't hurt us," Ma said. "You were a good girl, Laura, to do exactly as I told you, and to do it quickly, without asking why."

Ma was trembling, and she began to laugh

a little. "To think," she said, "I've slapped a bear!"

Then she put supper on the table for Laura and Mary. Pa had not come yet. He didn't come. Laura and Mary were undressed, and they said their prayers and snuggled into the trundle bed.

Ma sat by the lamp, mending one of Pa's shirts. The house seemed cold and still and strange, without Pa.

Laura listened to the wind in the Big Woods. All around the house the wind went crying as though it were lost in the dark and the cold. The wind sounded frightened.

Ma finished mending the shirt. Laura saw her fold it slowly and carefully. She smoothed it with her hand. Then she did a thing she had never done before. She went to the door and pulled the leather latch-string through its hole in the door, so that nobody could get in from outside unless she lifted the latch. She came and took Carrie, all limp and sleeping, out of the big bed.

She saw that Laura and Mary were still awake, and she said to them: "Go to sleep, girls. Everything is all right. Pa will be here in the morning."

Then she went back to her rocking chair and sat there rocking gently and holding Baby Carrie in her arms.

She was sitting up late, waiting for Pa, and Laura and Mary meant to stay awake, too, till he came. But at last they went to sleep.

In the morning Pa was there. He had brought candy for Laura and Mary, and two pieces of pretty calico to make them each a dress. Mary's was a china-blue pattern on a white ground, and Laura's was dark red with little golden-brown dots on it. Ma had calico for a dress, too; it was brown, with a big, feathery white pattern all over it.

They were all happy because Pa had got such good prices for his furs that he could afford to get them such beautiful presents.

The tracks of the big bear were all around the barn, and there were marks of his claws on the walls. But Sukey and the horses were safe inside.

All that day the sun shone, the snow melted, and little streams of water ran from the icicles, which all the time grew thinner. Before the sun set that night, the bear tracks were only shapeless marks in the wet, soft snow.

After supper Pa took Laura and Mary on his knees and said he had a new story to tell them.

THE STORY OF PA
AND THE BEAR IN THE WAY

"When I went to town yesterday with the furs I found it hard walking in the soft snow. It took me a long time to get to town, and other men with furs had come in earlier to do their trading. The storekeeper was busy, and I had to wait until he could look at my furs.

"Then we had to bargain about the price of each one, and then I had to pick out the things I wanted to take in trade.

"So it was nearly sundown before I could start home.

"I tried to hurry, but the walking was hard and I was tired, so I had not gone far before night came. And I was alone in the Big Woods without my gun.

"There were still six miles to walk, and I

came along as fast as I could. The night grew darker and darker, and I wished for my gun, because I knew that some of the bears had come out of their winter dens. I had seen their tracks when I went to town in the morning.

"Bears are hungry and cross at this time of year; you know they have been sleeping in their dens all winter long with nothing to eat, and that makes them thin and angry when they wake up. I did not want to meet one.

"I hurried along as quick as I could in the dark. By and by the stars gave a little light. It was still black as pitch where the woods were thick, but in the open places I could see, dimly. I could see the snowy road ahead a little way, and I could see the dark woods standing all around me. I was glad when I came into an open place where the stars gave me this faint light.

"All the time I was watching, as well as I could, for bears. I was listening for the sounds they make when they go carelessly through the bushes.

"Then I came again into an open place, and there, right in the middle of my road, I saw a big black bear.

"He was standing up on his hind legs, looking at me. I could see his eyes shine. I could see his pig-snout. I could even see one of his claws, in the starlight.

"My scalp prickled, and my hair stood straight up. I stopped in my tracks, and stood still. The bear did not move. There he stood, looking at me.

"I knew it would do no good to try to go around him. He would follow me into the dark woods, where he could see better than I could. I did not want to fight a winter-starved bear in the dark. Oh, how I wished for my gun!

"I had to pass that bear, to get home. I thought that if I could scare him, he might get out of the road and let me go by. So I took a deep breath, and suddenly I shouted with all my might and ran at him, waving my arms.

"He didn't move.

"I did not run very far toward him, I tell you! I stopped and looked at him, and he stood looking at me. Then I shouted again. There he stood. I kept on shouting and waving my arms, but he did not budge.

"Well, it would do me no good to run away. There were other bears in the woods. I might meet one any time. I might as well deal with this one as with another. Besides, I was coming home to Ma and you girls. I would never get here, if I ran away from everything in the woods that scared me.

"So at last I looked around, and I got a good big club, a solid, heavy branch that had been broken from a tree by the weight of snow in the winter.

"I lifted it up in my hands, and I ran straight at that bear. I swung my club as hard as I could and brought it down, bang! on his head.

"And there he still stood, for he was nothing but a big, black, burned stump!

"I had passed it on my way to town that morning. It wasn't a bear at all. I only thought it was a bear, because I had been thinking all the time about bears and being afraid I'd meet one."

"It really wasn't a bear at all?" Mary asked.

"No, Mary, it wasn't a bear at all. There I

had been yelling, and dancing, and waving my arms, all by myself in the Big Woods, trying to scare a stump!"

Laura said: "Ours was really a bear. But we were not scared, because we thought it was Sukey."

Pa did not say anything, but he hugged her tighter.

"Oo-oo! That bear might have eaten Ma and me all up!" Laura said, snuggling closer to him. "But Ma walked right up to him and slapped him, and he didn't do anything at all. Why didn't he do anything?"

"I guess he was too surprised to do anything, Laura," Pa said. "I guess he was afraid, when the lantern shone in his eyes. And when Ma walked up to him and slapped him, he knew *she* wasn't afraid."

"Well, you were brave, too," Laura said. "Even if it was only a stump, you thought it was a bear. You'd have hit him on the head with a club, if he *had* been a bear, wouldn't you, Pa?"

"Yes," said Pa, "I would. You see, I had to."

Then Ma said it was bedtime. She helped

Laura and Mary undress and button up their red flannel nightgowns. They knelt down by the trundle bed and said their prayers.

> *"Now I lay me down to sleep,*
> *I pray the Lord my soul to keep.*
> *If I should die before I wake,*
> *I pray the Lord my soul to take."*

Ma kissed them both, and tucked the covers in around them. They lay there awhile, looking at Ma's smooth, parted hair and her hands busy with sewing in the lamplight. Her needle made little clicking sounds against her thimble and then the thread went softly, swish! through the pretty calico that Pa had traded furs for.

Laura looked at Pa, who was greasing his boots. His mustaches and his hair and his long brown beard were silky in the lamplight, and the colors of his plaid jacket were gay. He whistled cheerfully while he worked, and then he sang:

"*The birds were singing in the morning,*
And the myrtle and the ivy were in bloom,
And the sun o'er the hills was a-dawning,
'Twas then that I laid her in the tomb."

It was a warm night. The fire had gone to coals on the hearth, and Pa did not build it up. All around the little house, in the Big Woods, there were little sounds of falling snow, and from the eaves there was the drip, drip of the melting icicles.

In just a little while the trees would be putting out their baby leaves, all rosy and yellow and pale green, and there would be wild flowers and birds in the woods.

Then there would be no more stories by the fire at night, but all day long Laura and Mary would run and play among the trees, for it would be spring.

THE SUGAR SNOW

For days the sun shone and the weather was warm. There was no frost on the windows in the mornings. All day the icicles fell one by one from the eaves with soft smashing and crackling sounds in the snowbanks beneath. The trees shook their wet, black branches, and chunks of snow fell down.

When Mary and Laura pressed their noses against the cold window pane they could see the drip of water from the eaves and the bare branches of the trees. The snow did not glitter;

it looked soft and tired. Under the trees it was pitted where the chunks of snow had fallen, and the banks beside the path were shrinking and settling.

Then one day Laura saw a patch of bare ground in the yard. All day it grew bigger, and before night the whole yard was bare mud. Only the icy path was left, and the snowbanks along the path and the fence and beside the woodpile.

"Can't I go out to play, Ma?" Laura asked, and Ma said:

"'May,' Laura."

"May I go out to play?" she asked.

"You may tomorrow," Ma promised.

That night Laura woke up, shivering. The bed-covers felt thin, and her nose was icy cold. Ma was tucking another quilt over her.

"Snuggle close to Mary," Ma said, "and you'll get warm."

In the morning the house was warm from the stove, but when Laura looked out of the window she saw that the ground was covered with soft, thick snow. All along the branches of the trees the snow was piled like feathers, and it lay in mounds along the top of the rail fence, and stood up in great, white balls on top of the gate-posts.

Pa came in, shaking the soft snow from his shoulders and stamping it from his boots.

"It's a sugar snow," he said.

Laura put her tongue quickly to a little bit of the white snow that lay in a fold of his sleeve. It was nothing but wet on her tongue, like any snow. She was glad that nobody had seen her taste it.

"Why is it a sugar snow, Pa?" she asked him, but he said he didn't have time to explain now. He must hurry away, he was going to Grandpa's.

Grandpa lived far away in the Big Woods, where the trees were closer together and larger.

Laura stood at the window and watched Pa, big and swift and strong, walking away over the snow. His gun was on his shoulder, his hatchet and powder horn hung at his side, and his tall boots made great tracks in the soft snow. Laura watched him till he was out of sight in the woods.

It was late before he came home that night. Ma had already lighted the lamp when he came in. Under one arm he carried a large package, and in the other hand was a big, covered, wooden bucket.

"Here, Caroline," he said, handing the package and the bucket to Ma, and then he put the gun on its hooks over the door.

"If I'd met a bear," he said, "I couldn't have shot him without dropping my load." Then he laughed. "And if I'd dropped that bucket and bundle, I wouldn't have had to shoot him. I could have stood and watched him eat what's in them and lick his chops."

Ma unwrapped the package and there were two hard, brown cakes, each as large as a milk pan. She uncovered the bucket, and it was full of dark brown syrup.

"Here, Laura and Mary," Pa said, and he gave them each a little round package out of his pocket.

They took off the paper wrappings, and each had a little, hard, brown cake, with beautifully crinkled edges.

"Bite it," said Pa, and his blue eyes twinkled.

Each bit off one little crinkle, and it was sweet. It crumbled in their mouths. It was better even than their Christmas candy.

"Maple sugar," said Pa.

Supper was ready, and Laura and Mary laid the little maple sugar cakes beside their plates, while they ate the maple syrup on their bread.

After supper, Pa took them on his knees as he sat before the fire, and told them about his day at Grandpa's, and the sugar snow.

"All winter," Pa said, "Grandpa has been making wooden buckets and little troughs. He made them of cedar and white ash, for those woods won't give a bad taste to the maple syrup.

"To make the troughs, he split out little sticks as long as my hand and as big as my two fingers. Near one end, Grandpa cut the stick half through, and split one half off. This left him a flat stick, with a square piece at one end. Then with a bit he bored a hole lengthwise through the square part, and with his knife he whittled the wood till it was only a thin shell around the round hole. The flat part of the stick he hollowed out with his knife till it was a little trough.

"He made dozens of them, and he made ten new wooden buckets. He had them all ready when the first warm weather came and the sap began to move in the trees.

"Then he went into the maple woods and with the bit he bored a hole in each maple tree, and he hammered the round end of the little trough into the hole, and he set a cedar bucket on the ground under the flat end.

"The sap, you know, is the blood of a tree. It comes up from the roots, when warm weather begins in the spring, and it goes to the very tip of each branch and twig, to make the green leaves grow.

"Well, when the maple sap came to the hole in the tree, it ran out of the tree, down the little trough and into the bucket."

"Oh, didn't it hurt the poor tree?" Laura asked.

"No more than it hurts you when you prick your finger and it bleeds," said Pa.

"Every day Grandpa puts on his boots and his warm coat and his fur cap and he goes out into the snowy woods and gathers the sap. With a barrel on a sled, he drives from tree to tree and empties the sap from the buckets into the barrel. Then he hauls it to a big iron kettle that hangs by a chain from a cross-timber between two trees.

"He empties the sap into the iron kettle. There is a big bonfire under the kettle, and the sap boils, and Grandpa watches it carefully. The fire must be hot enough to keep the sap boiling, but not hot enough to make it boil over.

"Every few minutes the sap must be skimmed. Grandpa skims it with a big, long-handled, wooden ladle that he made of basswood. When the sap gets too hot, Grandpa lifts ladlefuls of it high in the air and pours it back slowly. This cools the sap a little and keeps it from boiling too fast.

"When the sap has boiled down just enough, he fills the buckets with the syrup. After that, he boils the sap until it grains when he cools it in a saucer.

"The instant the sap is graining, Grandpa jumps to the fire and rakes it all out from beneath the kettle. Then as fast as he can, he ladles the thick syrup into the milk pans that are standing ready. In the pans the syrup turns to cakes of hard, brown maple sugar."

"So that's why it's a sugar snow, because Grandpa is making sugar?" Laura asked.

"No," Pa said. "It's called a sugar snow, because a snow this time of year means that men can make more sugar. You see, this little cold spell and the snow will hold back the leafing of the trees, and that makes a longer run of sap.

"When there's a long run of sap, it means that Grandpa can make enough maple sugar to last all the year, for common every day. When he takes his furs to town, he will not need to trade for much store sugar. He will get only a little store sugar, to have on the table when company comes."

"Grandpa must be glad there's a sugar snow," Laura said.

"Yes," Pa said, "he's very glad. He's going to sugar off again next Monday, and he says we must all come."

Pa's blue eyes twinkled; he had been saving the best for the last, and he said to Ma:

"Hey, Caroline! There'll be a dance!"

Ma smiled. She looked very happy, and she laid down her mending for a minute. "Oh, Charles!" she said.

Then she went on with her mending, but she kept on smiling. She said, "I'll wear my delaine."

Ma's delaine dress was beautiful. It was a dark green, with a little pattern all over it that looked like ripe strawberries. A dressmaker had made it, in the East, in the place where Ma came from when she married Pa and moved out west to the Big Woods in Wisconsin. Ma had been very fashionable, before she married Pa, and a dressmaker had made her clothes.

The delaine was kept wrapped in paper and laid away. Laura and Mary had never seen Ma wear it, but she had shown it to them once. She had let them touch the beautiful dark red buttons that buttoned the basque up the front, and she had shown them how neatly the whalebones were put in the seams, inside, with hundreds of little criss-cross stitches.

It showed how important a dance was, if Ma was going to wear the beautiful delaine dress. Laura and Mary were excited. They bounced up and down on Pa's knee, and asked questions about the dance until at last he said:

"Now you girls run along to bed! You'll know all about the dance when you see it. I have to put a new string on my fiddle."

There were sticky fingers and sweet mouths to be washed. Then there were prayers to be said. By the time Laura and Mary were snug in their trundle bed, Pa and the fiddle were both singing, while he kept time with his foot on the floor:

> *"I'm Captain Jinks of the Horse Marines,*
> *I feed my horse on corn and beans,*
> *And I often go beyond my means,*
> *For I'm Captain Jinks of the Horse Marines,*
> *I'm captain in the army!"*

DANCE AT GRANDPA'S

Monday morning everybody got up early, in a hurry to get started to Grandpa's. Pa wanted to be there to help with the work of gathering and boiling the sap. Ma would help Grandma and the aunts make good things to eat for all the people who were coming to the dance.

Breakfast was eaten and the dishes washed and the beds made by lamplight. Pa packed his fiddle carefully in its box and put it in the big sled that was already waiting at the gate.

The air was cold and frosty and the light

was gray, when Laura and Mary and Ma with Baby Carrie were tucked in snug and warm under the robes on the straw in the bottom of the sled.

The horses shook their heads and pranced, making the sleigh bells ring merrily, and away they went on the road through the Big Woods to Grandpa's.

The snow was damp and smooth in the road, so the sled slipped quickly over it, and the big trees seemed to be hurrying by on either side.

After a while there was sunshine in the woods and the air sparkled. The long streaks of yellow light lay between the shadows of the tree trunks, and the snow was colored faintly pink. All the shadows were thin and blue, and every little curve of snowdrifts and every little track in the snow had a shadow.

Pa showed Laura the tracks of the wild creatures in the snow at the sides of the road. The small, leaping tracks of cottontail rabbits, the tiny tracks of field mice, and the feather-stitching tracks of snowbirds. There were larger tracks, like dogs' tracks, where foxes had run, and there were the tracks of a deer that had bounded away into the woods.

The air was growing warmer already and Pa said that the snow wouldn't last long.

It did not seem long until they were sweeping into the clearing at Grandpa's house, all the sleigh bells jingling. Grandma came to the door and stood there smiling, calling to them to come in.

She said that Grandpa and Uncle George were already at work out in the maple woods. So Pa went to help them, while Laura and Mary and Ma, with Baby Carrie in her arms, went into Grandma's house and took off their wraps.

Laura loved Grandma's house. It was much larger than their house at home. There was one great big room, and then there was a little room that belonged to Uncle George, and there was another room for the aunts, Aunt Docia and Aunt Ruby. And then there was the kitchen, with a big cookstove.

It was fun to run the whole length of the big room, from the large fireplace at one end all the way to Grandma's bed, under the window in the other end. The floor was made of wide, thick slabs that Grandpa had hewed from the logs with his ax. The floor was smoothed all over, and scrubbed clean and white, and the big bed under the window was soft with feathers.

The day seemed very short while Laura and Mary played in the big room and Ma helped Grandma and the aunts in the kitchen. The men had taken their dinners to the maple woods, so for dinner they did not set the table, but ate cold venison sandwiches and drank milk. But for supper Grandma made hasty pudding.

She stood by the stove, sifting the yellow corn meal from her fingers into a kettle of boiling, salted water. She stirred the water all the time with a big wooden spoon, and sifted in the meal until the kettle was full of a thick, yellow, bubbling mass. Then she set it on the back of the stove where it would cook slowly.

It smelled good. The whole house smelled good, with the sweet and spicy smells from the kitchen, the smell of the hickory logs burning with clear, bright flames in the fireplace, and the smell of a clove-apple beside Grandma's mending basket on the table. The sunshine came in through the sparkling window panes, and everything was large and spacious and clean.

At supper time Pa and Grandpa came from the woods. Each had on his shoulders a wooden yoke that Grandpa had made. It was cut to fit around their necks in the back, and hollowed out to fit over their shoulders. From each end hung a chain with a hook, and on each hook hung a big wooden bucket full of hot maple syrup.

Pa and Grandpa had brought the syrup from the big kettle in the woods. They steadied the buckets with their hands, but the weight hung from the yokes on their shoulders.

Grandma made room for a huge brass kettle on the stove. Pa and Grandpa poured the syrup into the brass kettle, and it was so large that it held all the syrup from the four big buckets.

Then Uncle George came with a smaller bucket of syrup, and everybody ate the hot hasty pudding with maple syrup for supper.

Uncle George was home from the army. He wore his blue army coat with the brass buttons, and he had bold, merry blue eyes. He was big and broad and he walked with a swagger.

Laura looked at him all the time she was eating her hasty pudding, because she had heard Pa say to Ma that he was wild.

"George is wild, since he came back from the war," Pa had said, shaking his head as if he were sorry, but it couldn't be helped. Uncle George had run away to be a drummer boy in the army, when he was fourteen years old.

Laura had never seen a wild man before. She did not know whether she was afraid of Uncle George or not.

When supper was over, Uncle George went outside the door and blew his army bugle, long and loud. It made a lovely, ringing sound, far away through the Big Woods. The woods were dark and silent and the trees stood still as though they were listening. Then from very far away the sound came back, thin and clear and small, like a little bugle answering the big one.

"Listen," Uncle George said, "isn't that pretty?" Laura looked at him but she did not say anything, and when Uncle George stopped blowing the bugle she ran into the house.

Ma and Grandma cleared away the dishes and washed them, and swept the hearth, while Aunt Docia and Aunt Ruby made themselves pretty in their room.

Laura sat on their bed and watched them comb out their long hair and part it carefully. They parted it from their foreheads to the napes of their necks and then they parted it across from ear to ear. They braided their back hair in long braids and then they did the braids up carefully in big knots.

They had washed their hands and faces and scrubbed them well with soap, at the wash-basin on the bench in the kitchen. They had used store soap, not the slimy, soft, dark brown soap that Grandma made and kept in a big jar to use for common every day.

They fussed for a long time with their front hair, holding up the lamp and looking at their hair in the little looking-glass that hung on the log wall. They brushed it so smooth on each side of the straight white part that it shone like silk in the lamplight. The little puff on each side shone, too, and the ends were coiled and twisted neatly under the big knot in the back.

Then they pulled on their beautiful white stockings, that they had knit of fine cotton thread in lacy, openwork patterns, and they buttoned up their best shoes. They helped each other with their corsets. Aunt Docia pulled as hard as she could on Aunt Ruby's corset strings, and then Aunt Docia hung on to the foot of the bed while Aunt Ruby pulled on hers.

"Pull, Ruby, pull!" Aunt Docia said, breathless. "Pull harder." So Aunt Ruby braced her feet and pulled harder. Aunt Docia kept measuring her waist with her hands, and at last she gasped, "I guess that's the best you can do."

She said, "Caroline says Charles could span her waist with his hands, when they were married."

Caroline was Laura's Ma, and when she heard this Laura felt proud.

Then Aunt Ruby and Aunt Docia put on

their flannel petticoats and their plain petticoats and their stiff, starched white petticoats with knitted lace all around the flounces. And they put on their beautiful dresses.

Aunt Docia's dress was a sprigged print, dark blue, with sprigs of red flowers and green leaves thick upon it. The basque was buttoned down the front with black buttons which looked so exactly like juicy big blackberries that Laura wanted to taste them.

Aunt Ruby's dress was wine-colored calico, covered all over with a feathery pattern in lighter wine color. It buttoned with gold-colored buttons, and every button had a little castle and a tree carved on it.

Aunt Docia's pretty white collar was fastened in front with a large round cameo pin, which had a lady's head on it. But Aunt Ruby pinned her collar with a red rose made of sealing wax. She had made it herself, on the head of a darning needle which had a broken eye, so it couldn't be used as a needle any more.

They looked lovely, sailing over the floor so smoothly with their large, round skirts. Their little waists rose up tight and slender in the middle, and their cheeks were red and their eyes bright, under the wings of shining, sleek hair.

Ma was beautiful, too, in her dark green delaine, with the little leaves that looked like strawberries scattered over it. The skirt was ruffled and flounced and draped and trimmed with knots of dark green ribbon, and nestling at her throat was a gold pin. The pin was flat, as long and as wide as Laura's two biggest fingers, and it was carved all over, and scalloped on the edges. Ma looked so rich and fine that Laura was afraid to touch her.

People had begun to come. They were coming on foot through the snowy woods, with their lanterns, and they were driving up to the door in sleds and in wagons. Sleigh bells were jingling all the time.

The big room filled with tall boots and swishing skirts, and ever so many babies were lying in rows on Grandma's bed. Uncle James and Aunt Libby had come with their little girl, whose name was Laura Ingalls, too. The two

Lauras leaned on the bed and looked at the babies, and the other Laura said her baby was prettier than Baby Carrie.

"She is not, either!" Laura said. "Carrie's the prettiest baby in the whole world."

"No, she isn't," the other Laura said.

"Yes, she is!"

"No, she isn't!"

Ma came sailing over in her fine delaine, and said severely:

"Laura!"

So neither Laura said anything more.

Uncle George was blowing his bugle. It made a loud, ringing sound in the big room, and Uncle George joked and laughed and danced, blowing the bugle. Then Pa took his fiddle out of its box and began to play, and all the couples stood in squares on the floor and began to dance when Pa called the figures.

"Grand right and left!" Pa called out, and all the skirts began to swirl and all the boots began to stamp. The circles went round and round, all the skirts going one way and all the boots going the other way, and hands clasping and parting high up in the air.

"Swing your partners!" Pa called, and "Each gent bow to the lady on the left!"

They all did as Pa said. Laura watched Ma's skirt swaying and her little waist bending and her dark head bowing, and she thought Ma was the loveliest dancer in the world. The fiddle was singing:

> "Oh, you Buffalo gals,
>   Aren't you coming out tonight,
>   Aren't you coming out tonight,
>   Aren't you coming out tonight,
>   Oh, you Buffalo gals,
>   Aren't you coming out tonight,
>   To dance by the light of the moon?"

The little circles and the big circles went round and round, and the skirts swirled and the boots stamped, and partners bowed and separated and met and bowed again.

In the kitchen Grandma was all by herself, stirring the boiling syrup in the big brass kettle.

She stirred in time to the music. By the back door was a pail of clean snow, and sometimes Grandma took a spoonful of syrup from the kettle and poured it on some of the snow in a saucer.

Laura watched the dancers again. Pa was playing "The Irish Washerwoman" now. He called:

> *"Doe see, ladies, doe see doe,*
> *Come down heavy on your heel and toe!"*

Laura could not keep her feet still. Uncle George looked at her and laughed. Then he caught her by the hand and did a little dance with her, in the corner. She liked Uncle George.

Everybody was laughing, over by the kitchen door. They were dragging Grandma in from the kitchen. Grandma's dress was beautiful, too; a dark blue calico with autumn-colored leaves scattered over it. Her cheeks were pink from laughing, and she was shaking her head. The wooden spoon was in her hand.

"I can't leave the syrup," she said.

But Pa began to play "The Arkansas Traveler," and everybody began to clap in time to the music. So Grandma bowed to them all and did a few steps by herself. She could dance as prettily as any of them. The clapping almost drowned the music of Pa's fiddle.

Suddenly Uncle George did a pigeon wing, and bowing low before Grandma he began to jig. Grandma tossed her spoon to somebody. She put her hands on her hips and faced Uncle George, and everybody shouted. Grandma was jigging.

Laura clapped her hands in time to the music, with all the other clapping hands. The fiddle sang as it had never sung before. Grandma's eyes were snapping and her cheeks were red, and underneath her skirts her heels were clicking as fast as the thumping of Uncle George's boots.

Everybody was excited. Uncle George kept on jigging and Grandma kept on facing him, jigging too. The fiddle did not stop. Uncle George began to breathe loudly, and he wiped sweat off his forehead. Grandma's eyes twinkled.

"You can't beat her, George!" somebody shouted.

Uncle George jigged faster. He jigged twice as fast as he had been jigging. So did Grandma. Everybody cheered again. All the women were laughing and clapping their hands, and all the men were teasing George. George did not care, but he did not have breath enough to laugh. He was jigging.

Pa's blue eyes were snapping and sparking. He was standing up, watching George and Grandma, and the bow danced over the fiddle strings. Laura jumped up and down and squealed and clapped her hands.

Grandma kept on jigging. Her hands were on her hips and her chin was up and she was smiling. George kept on jigging, but his boots did not thump as loudly as they had thumped at first. Grandma's heels kept on clickety-clacking gaily. A drop of sweat dripped off George's forehead and shone on his cheek.

All at once he threw up both arms and gasped, "I'm beat!" He stopped jigging.

Everybody made a terrific noise, shouting and

yelling and stamping, cheering Grandma. Grandma jigged just a little minute more, then she stopped. She laughed in gasps. Her eyes sparkled just like Pa's when he laughed. George was laughing, too, and wiping his forehead on his sleeve.

Suddenly Grandma stopped laughing. She turned and ran as fast as she could into the kitchen. The fiddle had stopped playing. All the women were talking at once and all the men teasing George, but everybody was still for a minute, when Grandma looked like that.

Then she came to the door between the kitchen and the big room, and said:

"The syrup is waxing. Come and help yourselves."

Then everybody began to talk and laugh again. They all hurried to the kitchen for plates, and outdoors to fill the plates with snow. The kitchen door was open and the cold air came in.

Outdoors the stars were frosty in the sky and the air nipped Laura's cheeks and nose. Her breath was like smoke.

She and the other Laura, and all the other

children, scooped up clean snow with their plates. Then they went back into the crowded kitchen.

Grandma stood by the brass kettle and with the big wooden spoon she poured hot syrup on each plate of snow. It cooled into soft candy, and as fast as it cooled they ate it.

They could eat all they wanted, for maple sugar never hurt anybody. There was plenty of syrup in the kettle, and plenty of snow outdoors. As soon as they ate one plateful, they filled their plates with snow again, and Grandma poured more syrup on it.

When they had eaten the soft maple candy until they could eat no more of it, then they helped themselves from the long table loaded with pumpkin pies and dried berry pies and cookies and cakes. There was salt-rising bread, too, and cold boiled pork, and pickles. Oo, how sour the pickles were!

They all ate till they could hold no more, and then they began to dance again. But Grandma watched the syrup in the kettle. Many times she took a little of it out into a saucer, and stirred it round and round. Then she shook her head and poured the syrup back into the kettle.

The other room was loud and merry with the music of the fiddle and the noise of the dancing.

At last, as Grandma stirred, the syrup in the saucer turned into little grains like sand, and Grandma called:

"Quick, girls! It's graining!"

Aunt Ruby and Aunt Docia and Ma left the dance and came running. They set out pans, big pans and little pans, and as fast as Grandma filled them with the syrup they set out more. They set the filled ones away, to cool into maple sugar.

Then Grandma said:

"Now bring the patty-pans for the children."

There was a patty-pan, or at least a broken cup or a saucer, for every little girl and boy. They all watched anxiously while Grandma ladled out the syrup. Perhaps there would not be enough. Then somebody would have to be unselfish and polite.

There was just enough syrup to go round.

The last scrapings of the brass kettle exactly filled the very last patty-pan. Nobody was left out.

The fiddling and the dancing went on and on. Laura and the other Laura stood around and watched the dancers. Then they sat down on the floor in a corner, and watched. The dancing was so pretty and the music so gay that Laura knew she could never get tired of it.

All the beautiful skirts went swirling by, and the boots went stamping, and the fiddle kept on singing gaily.

Then Laura woke up, and she was lying across the foot of Grandma's bed. It was morning. Ma and Grandma and Baby Carrie were in the bed. Pa and Grandpa were sleeping rolled up in blankets on the floor by the fireplace. Mary was nowhere in sight; she was sleeping with Aunt Docia and Aunt Ruby in their bed.

Soon everybody was getting up. There were pancakes and maple syrup for breakfast, and then Pa brought the horses and sled to the door.

He helped Ma and Carrie in, while Grandpa

picked up Mary and Uncle George picked up Laura and they tossed them over the edge of the sled into the straw. Pa tucked in the robes around them, and Grandpa and Grandma and Uncle George stood calling, "Good-by! Good-by!" as they rode away into the Big Woods, going home.

The sun was warm, and the trotting horses threw up bits of muddy snow with their hoofs. Behind the sled Laura could see their footprints, and every footprint had gone through the thin snow into the mud.

"Before night," Pa said, "we'll see the last of the sugar snow."

GOING TO TOWN

After the sugar snow had gone, spring came. Birds sang in the leafing hazel bushes along the crooked rail fence. The grass grew green again and the woods were full of wild flowers. Buttercups and violets, thimble flowers and tiny starry grassflowers were everywhere.

As soon as the days were warm, Laura and Mary begged to be allowed to run barefoot. At first they might only run out around the woodpile and back, in their bare feet. Next day they could run farther, and soon their shoes were oiled and put away and they ran barefoot all day long.

Every night they had to wash their feet before they went to bed. Under the hems of their skirts their ankles and their feet were as brown as their faces.

They had playhouses under the two big oak trees in front of the house. Mary's playhouse was under Mary's tree, and Laura's playhouse was under Laura's tree. The soft grass made a green carpet for them. The green leaves were the roofs, and through them they could see bits of the blue sky.

Pa made a swing of tough bark and hung it to a large, low branch of Laura's tree. It was her swing because it was in her tree, but she had to be unselfish and let Mary swing in it whenever she wanted to.

Mary had a cracked saucer to play with, and Laura had a beautiful cup with only one big piece broken out of it. Charlotte and Nettie, and the two little wooden men Pa had made, lived in the playhouse with them. Every day they made fresh leaf hats for Charlotte and Nettie, and they made little leaf cups and saucers to set on their table. The table was a nice, smooth rock.

Sukey and Rosie, the cows, were turned loose in the woods now, to eat the wild grass and the juicy new leaves. There were two little calves in the barnyard, and seven little pigs with the mother hog in the pigpen.

In the clearing he had made last year, Pa was plowing around the stumps and putting in his crops. One night he came in from work and said to Laura:

"What do you think I saw today?"

She couldn't guess.

"Well," Pa said. "When I was working in the clearing this morning, I looked up, and there at the edge of the woods stood a deer. She was a doe, a mother deer, and you'll never guess what was with her!"

"A baby deer!" Laura and Mary guessed together, clasping their hands.

"Yes," Pa said, "her fawn was with her. It

was a pretty little thing, the softest fawn color, with big dark eyes. It had the tiniest feet, not much bigger than my thumb, and it had slender little legs, and the softest muzzle.

"It stood there and looked at me with its large, soft eyes, wondering what I was. It was not afraid at all."

"You wouldn't shoot a little baby deer, would you, Pa?" Laura said.

"No, never!" he answered. "Nor its Ma, nor its Pa. No more hunting, now, till all the little wild animals have grown up. We'll just have to do without fresh meat till fall."

Pa said that as soon as he had the crops in, they would all go to town. Laura and Mary could go, too. They were old enough now.

They were very much excited, and next day they tried to play going to town. They could not do it very well, because they were not quite sure what a town was like. They knew there was a store in town, but they had never seen a store.

Nearly every day after that, Charlotte and

Nettie would ask if they could go to town. But Laura and Mary always said: "No, dear, you can't go this year. Perhaps next year, if you are good, then you can go."

Then one night Pa said, "We'll go to town tomorrow."

That night, though it was the middle of the week, Ma bathed Laura and Mary all over, and she put up their hair. She divided their long hair into wisps, combed each wisp with a wet comb and wound it tightly on a bit of rag. There were knobby little bumps all over their heads, whichever way they turned on their pillows. In the morning their hair would be curly.

They were so excited that they did not go to sleep at once. Ma was not sitting with her mending basket as usual. She was busy getting everything ready for a quick breakfast and laying out the best stockings and petticoats and dresses, and Pa's good shirt, and her own dark brown calico with the little purple flowers on it.

The days were longer now. In the morning

Ma blew out the lamp before they finished breakfast. It was a beautiful, clear spring morning.

Ma hurried Laura and Mary with their breakfast and she washed the dishes quickly. They put on their stockings and shoes while she made the beds. Then she helped them put on their best dresses—Mary's china-blue calico and Laura's dark red calico. Mary buttoned Laura up the back, and then Ma buttoned Mary.

Ma took the rags off their hair and combed it into long, round curls that hung down over their shoulders. She combed so fast that the snarls hurt dreadfully. Mary's hair was beautifully golden, but Laura's was only a dirt-colored brown.

When their curls were done, Ma tied their sunbonnets under their chins. She fastened her collar with the gold pin, and she was putting on her hat when Pa drove up to the gate.

He had curried the horses till they shone. He had swept the wagon box clean and laid a clean blanket on the wagon seat. Ma, with

Baby Carrie in her arms, sat up on the wagon seat with Pa, and Laura and Mary sat on a board fastened across the wagon box behind the seat.

They were happy as they drove through the springtime woods. Carrie laughed and bounced, Ma was smiling, and Pa whistled while he drove the horses. The sun was bright and warm on the road. Sweet, cool smells came out of the leafy woods.

Rabbits stood up in the road ahead, their little front paws dangling down and their noses sniffing, and the sun shone through their tall, twitching ears. Then they bounded away, with a flash of little white tail. Twice Laura and Mary saw deer looking at them with their large, dark eyes, from the shadows among the trees.

It was seven miles to town. The town was named Pepin, and it was on the shore of Lake Pepin.

After a long time Laura began to see glimpses of blue water between the trees. The hard road turned to soft sand. The wagon wheels went deep down in it and the horses pulled and sweated. Often Pa stopped them to rest for a few minutes.

Then all at once the road came out of the woods and Laura saw the lake. It was as blue as the sky, and it went to the edge of the world. As far as she could see, there was nothing but flat, blue water. Very far away, the sky and the water met, and there was a darker blue line.

The sky was large overhead. Laura had never known that the sky was so big. There was so much empty space all around her that she felt small and frightened, and glad that Pa and Ma were there.

Suddenly the sunshine was hot. The sun was almost overhead in the large, empty sky, and the cool woods stood back from the edge of the lake. Even the Big Woods seemed smaller under so much sky.

Pa stopped the horses, and turned around on the wagon seat. He pointed ahead with his whip.

"There you are, Laura and Mary!" he said. "There's the town of Pepin."

Laura stood up on the board and Pa held her safe by the arm, so she could see the town. When she saw it, she could hardly breathe. She knew how Yankee Doodle felt, when he could not see the town because there were so many houses.

Right on the edge of the lake, there was one great big building. That was the store, Pa told her. It was not made of logs. It was made of wide, gray boards, running up and down. The sand spread all around it.

Behind the store there was a clearing, larger than Pa's clearing in the woods at home. Standing among the stumps, there were more houses than Laura could count. They were not made of logs, either; they were made of boards, like the store.

Laura had never imagined so many houses, and they were so close together. Of course, they were much smaller than the store. One of them was made of new boards that had not had time to get gray; it was the yellow color of newly-cut wood.

People were living in all these houses. Smoke

rose up from their chimneys. Though it was not Monday, some woman had spread out a washing on the bushes and stumps by her house.

Several girls and boys were playing in the sunshine, in the open space between the store and the houses. They were jumping from one stump to the next stump and shouting.

"Well, that's Pepin," Pa said.

Laura just nodded her head. She looked and looked, and could not say a word. After a while she sat down again, and the horses went on.

They left the wagon on the shore of the lake. Pa unhitched the horses and tied one to each side of the wagon box. Then he took Laura and Mary by the hand, and Ma came beside them carrying Baby Carrie. They walked through the deep sand to the store. The warm sand came in over the tops of Laura's shoes.

There was a wide platform in front of the store, and at one end of it steps went up to it out of the sand. Laura's heart was beating so fast that she could hardly climb the steps. She was trembling all over.

This was the store to which Pa came to trade his furs. When they went in, the storekeeper knew him. The storekeeper came out from behind the counter and spoke to him and to Ma, and then Laura and Mary had to show their manners.

Mary said, "How do you do?" but Laura could not say anything.

The storekeeper said to Pa and Ma, "That's a pretty little girl you've got there," and he admired Mary's golden curls. But he did not say anything about Laura, or about her curls. They were ugly and brown.

The store was full of things to look at. All along one side of it were shelves full of colored prints and calicos. There were beautiful pinks and blues and reds and browns and purples. On the floor along the sides of the plank counters there were kegs of nails, and kegs of round, gray shot, and there were big wooden pails full of candy. There were sacks of salt, and sacks of store sugar.

In the middle of the store was a plow made

of shiny wood, with a glittering bright plow-share, and there were steel ax heads, and hammer heads, and saws, and all kinds of knives—hunting knives and skinning knives and butcher knives and jack-knives. There were big boots and little boots, big shoes and little shoes.

Laura could have looked for weeks and not seen all the things that were in that store. She had not known there were so many things in the world.

Pa and Ma traded for a long time. The storekeeper took down bolts and bolts of beau-tiful calicos and spread them out for Ma to finger and look at and price. Laura and Mary looked, but must not touch. Every new color and pattern was prettier than the last, and there were so many of them! Laura did not know how Ma could ever choose.

Ma chose two patterns of calico to make shirts for Pa, and a piece of brown denim to make him a jumper. Then she got some white cloth to make sheets and underwear.

Pa got enough calico to make Ma a new apron. Ma said:

"Oh, no, Charles, I don't really need it."

But Pa laughed and said she must pick it out, or he would get her the turkey red piece with the big yellow pattern. Ma smiled and flushed pink, and she picked out a pattern of rosebuds and leaves on a soft, fawn-colored ground.

Then Pa got for himself a pair of galluses and some tobacco to smoke in his pipe. And Ma got a pound of tea, and a little paper package of store sugar to have in the house when company came. It was a pale brown sugar, not dark brown like the maple sugar Ma used for every day.

When all the trading was done, the storekeeper gave Mary and Laura each a piece of candy. They were so astonished and so pleased that they just stood looking at their candies. Then Mary remembered and said, "Thank you."

Laura could not speak. Everybody was waiting, and she could not make a sound. Ma had to ask her:

"What do you say, Laura?"

Then Laura opened her mouth and gulped and whispered, "Thank you."

After that they went out of the store. Both pieces of candy were white, and flat and thin and heart-shaped. There was printing on them, in red letters. Ma read it for them. Mary's said:

> *Roses are red*
> *Violets are blue,*
> *Sugar is sweet,*
> *And so are you.*

Laura's said only:

> *Sweets to the sweet.*

The pieces of candy were exactly the same size. Laura's printing was larger than Mary's.

They all went back through the sand to the wagon on the lake shore. Pa fed the horses, on the bottom of the wagon box, some oats he had brought for their dinner. Ma opened the picnic box.

They all sat on the warm sand near the wagon

and ate bread and butter and cheese, hard-boiled eggs and cookies. The waves of Lake Pepin curled up on the shore at their feet and slid back with the smallest hissing sound.

After dinner, Pa went back to the store to talk awhile with other men. Ma sat holding Carrie quietly until she went to sleep. But Laura and Mary ran along the lake shore, picking up pretty pebbles that had been rolled back and forth by the waves until they were polished smooth.

There were no pebbles like that in the Big Woods.

When she found a pretty one, Laura put it in her pocket, and there were so many, each prettier than the last, that she filled her pocket full. Then Pa called, and they ran back to the wagon, for the horses were hitched up and it was time to go home.

Laura was so happy, when she ran through the sand to Pa, with all those beautiful pebbles in her pocket. But when Pa picked her up and tossed her into the wagon, a dreadful thing happened.

The heavy pebbles tore her pocket right out

of her dress. The pocket fell, and the pebbles rolled all over the bottom of the wagon box.

Laura cried because she had torn her best dress.

Ma gave Carrie to Pa and came quickly to look at the torn place. Then she said it was all right.

"Stop crying, Laura," she said. "I can fix it." She showed Laura that the dress was not torn at all, nor the pocket. The pocket was a little bag, sewed into the seam of the dress skirt, and hanging under it. Only the seams had ripped. Ma could sew the pocket in again, as good as new.

"Pick up the pretty pebbles, Laura," Ma said. "And another time, don't be so greedy."

So Laura gathered up the pebbles, put them in the pocket, and carried the pocket in her lap. She did not mind very much when Pa laughed at her for being such a greedy little girl that she took more than she could carry away.

Nothing like that ever happened to Mary. Mary was a good little girl who always kept her dress clean and neat and minded her manners. Mary had lovely golden curls, and her candy heart had a poem on it.

Mary looked very good and sweet, un-rumpled and clean, sitting on the board beside Laura. Laura did not think it was fair.

But it had been a wonderful day, the most wonderful day in her whole life. She thought about the beautiful lake, and the town she had seen, and the big store full of so many things. She held the pebbles carefully in her lap, and her candy heart wrapped carefully in her hand-kerchief until she got home and could put it away to keep always. It was too pretty to eat.

The wagon jolted along on the homeward road through the Big Woods. The sun set, and the woods grew darker, but before the last of the twilight was gone the moon rose. And they were safe, because Pa had his gun.

The soft moonlight came down through the treetops and made patches of light and shade on the road ahead. The horses' hoofs made a cheerful clippety-clop.

Laura and Mary did not say anything because they were very tired, and Ma sat silently holding Baby Carrie, sleeping in her arms. But Pa sang softly:

"'Mid pleasures and palaces,
    though we may roam,
Be it ever so humble,
    there's no place like home."

SUMMERTIME

N ow it was summertime, and people went visiting. Sometimes Uncle Henry, or Uncle George, or Grandpa, came riding out of the Big Woods to see Pa. Ma would come to the door and ask how all the folks were, and she would say:

"Charles is in the clearing."

Then she would cook more dinner than usual, and dinner time would be longer. Pa and Ma and the visitor would sit talking a little while before they went back to work.

Sometimes Ma let Laura and Mary go across the road and down the hill, to see Mrs. Peterson. The Petersons had just moved in. Their house was new, and always very neat, because Mrs. Peterson had no little girls to muss it up. She was a Swede, and she let Laura and Mary look at the pretty things she had brought from Sweden—laces, and colored embroideries, and china.

Mrs. Peterson talked Swedish to them, and they talked English to her, and they understood each other perfectly. She always gave them each a cookie when they left, and they nibbled the cookies very slowly while they walked home.

Laura nibbled away exactly half of hers, and Mary nibbled exactly half of hers, and the other halves they saved for Baby Carrie. Then when they got home, Carrie had two half-cookies, and that was a whole cookie.

This wasn't right. All they wanted to do was to divide the cookies fairly with Carrie. Still, if Mary saved half her cookie, while Laura ate the whole of hers, or if Laura saved half, and Mary ate her whole cookie, that wouldn't be fair, either.

They didn't know what to do. So each saved half, and gave it to Baby Carrie. But they always felt that somehow that wasn't quite fair.

Sometimes a neighbor sent word that the family was coming to spend the day. Then Ma did extra cleaning and cooking, and opened the package of store sugar. And on the day set, a wagon would come driving up to the gate in the morning and there would be strange children to play with.

When Mr. and Mrs. Huleatt came, they brought Eva and Clarence with them. Eva was a pretty girl, with dark eyes and black curls. She played carefully and kept her dress clean and smooth. Mary liked that, but Laura liked better to play with Clarence.

Clarence was red-headed and freckled, and always laughing. His clothes were pretty, too. He wore a blue suit buttoned all the way up the front with bright gilt buttons, and trimmed with braid, and he had copper-toed shoes.

The strips of copper across the toes were so glittering bright that Laura wished she were a boy. Little girls didn't wear copper-toes.

Laura and Clarence ran and shouted and climbed trees, while Mary and Eva walked nicely together and talked. Ma and Mrs. Huleatt visited and looked at a *Godey's Lady's Book* which Mrs. Huleatt had brought, and Pa and Mr. Huleatt looked at the horses and the crops and smoked their pipes.

Once Aunt Lotty came to spend the day. That morning Laura had to stand still a long time while Ma unwound her hair from the cloth strings and combed it into long curls. Mary was all ready, sitting primly on a chair, with her golden curls shining and her china-blue dress fresh and crisp.

Laura liked her own red dress. But Ma pulled her hair dreadfully, and it was brown instead of golden, so that no one noticed it. Everyone noticed and admired Mary's.

"There!" Ma said at last. "Your hair is curled beautifully, and Lotty is coming. Run meet her, both of you, and ask her which she likes best, brown curls or golden curls."

Laura and Mary ran out of the door and down the path, for Aunt Lotty was already at the gate. Aunt Lotty was a big girl, much taller than Mary. Her dress was a beautiful pink and she was swinging a pink sunbonnet by one string.

"Which do you like best, Aunt Lotty," Mary asked, "brown curls, or golden curls?" Ma had told them to ask that, and Mary was a very good little girl who always did exactly as she was told.

Laura waited to hear what Aunt Lotty would say, and she felt miserable.

"I like both kinds best," Aunt Lotty said, smiling. She took Laura and Mary by the hand, one on either side, and they danced along to the door where Ma stood.

The sunshine came streaming through the windows into the house, and everything was so neat and pretty. The table was covered with a red cloth, and the cookstove was polished shining black. Through the bedroom door Laura could see the trundle bed in its place under the big bed. The pantry door stood wide open, giving the sight and smell of goodies on the shelves, and Black Susan came purring down the stairs from the attic, where she had been taking a nap.

It was all so pleasant, and Laura felt so gay and good that no one would ever have thought she could be as naughty as she was that evening.

Aunt Lotty had gone, and Laura and Mary were tired and cross. They were at the wood-pile, gathering a pan of chips to kindle the fire in the morning. They always hated to pick up chips, but every day they had to do it. Tonight they hated it more than ever.

Laura grabbed the biggest chip, and Mary said:

"I don't care. Aunt Lotty likes my hair best, anyway. Golden hair is lots prettier than brown."

Laura's throat swelled tight, and she could not speak. She knew golden hair was prettier than brown. She couldn't speak, so she reached out quickly and slapped Mary's face.

Then she heard Pa say, "Come here, Laura."

She went slowly, dragging her feet. Pa was sitting just inside the door. He had seen her slap Mary.

"You remember," Pa said, "I told you girls you must never strike each other."

Laura began, "But Mary said—"

"That makes no difference," said Pa. "It is what I say that you must mind."

Then he took down a strap from the wall, and he whipped Laura with the strap.

Laura sat on a chair in the corner and sobbed. When she stopped sobbing, she sulked. The only thing in the whole world to be glad about was that Mary had to fill the chip pan all by herself.

At last, when it was getting dark, Pa said again, "Come here, Laura." His voice was kind, and when Laura came he took her on his knee and hugged her close. She sat in the crook of his arm, her head against his shoulder and his long brown whiskers partly covering her eyes, and everything was all right again.

She told Pa all about it, and she asked him, "You don't like golden hair better than brown, do you?"

Pa's blue eyes shone down at her, and he said, "Well, Laura, my hair is brown."

She had not thought of that. Pa's hair was brown, and his whiskers were brown, and she thought brown was a lovely color. But she was glad that Mary had had to gather all the chips.

In the summer evenings Pa did not tell stories or play the fiddle. Summer days were long, and he was tired after he had worked hard all day in the fields.

Ma was busy, too. Laura and Mary helped her weed the garden, and they helped her feed the calves and the hens. They gathered the eggs, and they helped make cheese.

When the grass was tall and thick in the woods and the cows were giving plenty of milk, that was the time to make cheese.

Somebody must kill a calf, for cheese could not be made without rennet, and rennet is the lining of a young calf's stomach. The calf must be very young, so that it had never eaten anything but milk.

Laura was afraid that Pa must kill one of the little calves in the barn. They were so sweet. One was fawn-colored and one was red, and their hair was so soft and their large eyes so wondering. Laura's heart beat fast when Ma talked to Pa about making cheese.

Pa would not kill either of his calves, because they were heifers and would grow into cows. He went to Grandpa's and to Uncle Henry's, to talk about the cheese-making, and Uncle Henry said he would kill one of his calves. There would be enough rennet for Aunt Polly and Grandma and Ma.

So Pa went again to Uncle Henry's, and came back with a piece of the little calf's stomach. It was like a piece of soft, grayish-white leather, all ridged and rough on one side.

When the cows were milked at night, Ma set the milk away in pans. In the morning she skimmed off the cream to make into butter later. Then when the morning's milk had cooled, she mixed it with the skimmed milk and set it all on the stove to heat.

A bit of the rennet, tied in a cloth, was soaking in warm water.

When the milk was heated enough, Ma squeezed every drop of water from the rennet in the cloth, and then she poured the water into the milk. She stirred it well and left it in a warm place by the stove. In a little while it thickened into a smooth, quivery mass.

With a long knife Ma cut this mass into little squares, and let it stand while the curd separated from the whey. Then she poured it all into a cloth and let the thin, yellowish whey drain out.

When no more whey dripped from the cloth, Ma emptied the curd into a big pan and salted it, turning and mixing it well.

Laura and Mary were always there, helping all they could. They loved to eat bits of the curd when Ma was salting it. It squeaked in their teeth.

Under the cherry tree outside the back door Pa had put up the board to press the cheese on. He had cut two grooves the length of the board, and laid the board on blocks, one end a little higher than the other. Under the lower end stood an empty pail.

Ma put her wooden cheese hoop on the board, spread a clean, wet cloth all over the inside of it, and filled it heaping full of the chunks of salted curd. She covered this with another clean, wet cloth, and laid on top of it a round board, cut small enough to go inside the cheese hoop. Then she lifted a heavy rock on top of the board.

All day long the round board settled slowly under the weight of the rock, and whey pressed out and ran down the grooves of the board into the pail.

Next morning, Ma would take out the round, pale yellow cheese, as large as a milk pan. Then she made more curd, and filled the cheese hoop again.

Every morning she took the new cheese out of the press, and trimmed it smooth. She sewed a cloth tightly around it, and rubbed the cloth all over with fresh butter. Then she put the cheese on a shelf in the pantry.

Every day she wiped every cheese carefully with a wet cloth, then rubbed it all over with fresh butter once more, and laid it down on its other side. After a great many days, the cheese was ripe, and there was a hard rind all over it.

Then Ma wrapped each cheese in paper and laid it away on the high shelf. There was nothing more to do with it but eat it.

Laura and Mary liked cheese-making. They liked to eat the curd that squeaked in their teeth and they liked to eat the edges Ma pared off the big, round, yellow cheeses to make them smooth, before she sewed them up in cloth.

Ma laughed at them for eating green cheese.

"The moon is made of green cheese, some people say," she told them.

The new cheese did look like the round moon when it came up behind the trees. But it was not green; it was yellow, like the moon.

"It's green," Ma said, "because it isn't ripened yet. When it's cured and ripened, it won't be a green cheese."

"Is the moon really made of green cheese?" Laura asked, and Ma laughed.

"I think people say that, because it looks like a green cheese," she said. "But appearances are deceiving." Then while she wiped all the green cheeses and rubbed them with butter, she told them about the dead, cold moon that is like a little world on which nothing grows.

The first day Ma made cheese, Laura tasted the whey. She tasted it without saying anything to Ma, and when Ma turned around and saw her face, Ma laughed. That night while she was washing the supper dishes and Mary and Laura were wiping them, Ma told Pa that Laura had tasted the whey and didn't like it.

"You wouldn't starve to death on Ma's whey, like old Grimes did on his wife's," Pa said.

Laura begged him to tell her about Old Grimes. So, though Pa was tired, he took his fiddle out of its box and played and sang for Laura:

> *"Old Grimes is dead, that good old man,*
> *We ne'er shall see him more,*
> *He used to wear an old gray coat,*
> *All buttoned down before.*

"Old Grimes's wife made skim-milk cheese,
Old Grimes, he drank the whey,
There came an east wind from the west,
And blew Old Grimes away."

"There you have it!" said Pa. "She was a mean, tight-fisted woman. If she hadn't skimmed all the milk, a little cream would have run off in the whey, and Old Grimes might have staggered along.

"But she skimmed off every bit of cream, and poor Old Grimes got so thin the wind blew him away. Plumb starved to death."

Then Pa looked at Ma and said, "Nobody'd starve to death when you were around, Caroline."

"Well, no," Ma said. "No, Charles, not if you were there to provide for us."

Pa was pleased. It was all so pleasant, the doors and windows wide open to the summer evening, the dishes making little cheerful sounds together as Ma washed them and Mary and Laura wiped, and Pa putting away the fiddle and smiling and whistling softly to himself.

After a while he said, "I'm going over to Henry's tomorrow morning, Caroline, to borrow his grubbing hoe. Those sprouts are getting waist-high around the stumps in the wheat-field. A man just has to keep everlasting at it, or the woods'll take back the place."

Early next morning he started to walk to Uncle Henry's. But before long he came hurrying back, hitched the horses to the wagon, threw in his ax, the two washtubs, the washboiler and all the pails and wooden buckets there were.

"I don't know if I'll need 'em all, Caroline," he said, "but I'd hate to want 'em and not have 'em."

"Oh what is it? What is it?" Laura asked, jumping up and down with excitement.

"Pa's found a bee tree," Ma said. "Maybe he'll bring us some honey."

It was noon before Pa came driving home. Laura had been watching for him, and she ran out to the wagon as soon as it stopped by the barnyard. But she could not see into it.

Pa called, "Caroline, if you'll come take this pail of honey, I'll go unhitch."

Ma came out to the wagon, disappointed. She said:

"Well, Charles, even a pail of honey is something." Then she looked into the wagon and threw up her hands. Pa laughed.

All the pails and buckets were heaping full of dripping, golden honeycomb. Both tubs were piled full, and so was the wash-boiler.

Pa and Ma went back and forth, carrying the two loaded tubs and the wash-boiler and all the buckets and pails into the house. Ma heaped a plate high with the golden pieces, and covered all the rest neatly with cloths.

For dinner they all had as much of the delicious honey as they could eat, and Pa told them how he found the bee tree.

"I didn't take my gun," he said, "because I wasn't hunting, and now it's summer there wasn't much danger of meeting trouble. Panthers and bears are so fat, this time of year, that they're lazy and good-natured.

"Well, I took a short cut through the woods, and I nearly ran into a big bear. I came around a clump of underbrush, and there he was, not as far from me as across this room.

"He looked around at me, and I guess he saw I didn't have a gun. Anyway, he didn't pay any more attention to me.

"He was standing at the foot of a big tree, and bees were buzzing all around him. They couldn't sting through his thick fur, and he kept brushing them away from his head with one paw.

"I stood there watching him, and he put the other paw into a hole in the tree and drew it out all dripping with honey. He licked the honey off his paw and reached in for more. But by that time I had found me a club. I wanted that honey myself.

"So I made a great racket, banging the club against a tree and yelling. The bear was so fat and so full of honey that he just dropped on all fours and waddled off among the trees. I chased him some distance and got him going fast, away from the bee tree, and then I came back for the wagon."

Laura asked him how he got the honey away from the bees.

"That was easy," Pa said. "I left the horses back in the woods, where they wouldn't get stung, and then I chopped the tree down and split it open."

"Didn't the bees sting you?"

"No," said Pa. "Bees never sting me.

"The whole tree was hollow, and filled from top to bottom with honey. The bees must have been storing honey there for years. Some of it was old and dark, but I guess I got enough good, clean honey to last us a long time."

Laura was sorry for the poor bees. She said:

"They worked so hard, and now they won't have any honey."

But Pa said there was lots of honey left for the bees, and there was another large, hollow tree near by, into which they could move. He said it was time they had a clean, new home.

They would take the old honey he had left

in the old tree, make it into fresh, new honey, and store it in their new house. They would save every drop of the spilled honey and put it away, and they would have plenty of honey again, long before winter came.

HARVEST

Pa and Uncle Henry traded work. When the grain got ripe in the fields, Uncle Henry came to work with Pa, and Aunt Polly and all the cousins came to spend the day. Then Pa went to help Uncle Henry cut his grain, and Ma took Laura and Mary and Carrie to spend the day with Aunt Polly.

Ma and Aunt Polly worked in the house and all the cousins played together in the yard till dinner time. Aunt Polly's yard was a fine place to play, because the stumps were so thick. The cousins played jumping from stump to stump without ever touching the ground.

Even Laura, who was littlest, could do this easily in the places where the smallest trees had grown close together. Cousin Charley was a big boy, going on eleven years old, and he could jump from stump to stump all over the yard. The smaller stumps he could jump two at a time, and he could walk on the top rail of the fence without being afraid.

Pa and Uncle Henry were out in the field, cutting the oats with cradles. A cradle was a sharp steel blade fastened to a framework of wooden slats that caught and held the stalks of grain when the blade cut them. Pa and Uncle Henry carried the cradles by their long, curved handles, and swung the blades into the standing oats. When they had cut enough to make a pile, they slid the cut stalks off the slats, into neat heaps on the ground.

It was hard work, walking around and around the field in the hot sun, and with both hands swinging the heavy cradles into the grain and cutting it, then sliding it into the piles.

After all the grain was cut, they must go

over the field again. This time they would stoop over each pile, and taking up a handful of the stalks in each hand they would knot them together to make a longer strand. Then gathering up the pile of grain in their arms they would bind it tightly around with the band they had made, and tie the band, and tuck in its ends.

After they made seven such bundles, then the bundles must be shocked. To make a shock, they stood five bundles upright, snugly together with the oat-heads up. Then over these they put two more bundles, spreading out the stalks to make a little roof and shelter the five bundles from dew and rain.

Every stalk of the cut grain must always be safely in the shock before dark, for lying on the dewy ground all night would spoil it.

Pa and Uncle Henry were working very hard, because the air was so heavy and hot and still that they expected rain. The oats were ripe, and if they were not cut and in the shock before rain came, the crop would be lost. Then Uncle Henry's horses would be hungry all winter.

At noon Pa and Uncle Henry came to the house in a great hurry, and swallowed their dinner as quickly as they could. Uncle Henry said that Charley must help them that afternoon.

Laura looked at Pa, when Uncle Henry said that. At home, Pa had said to Ma that Uncle Henry and Aunt Polly spoiled Charley. When Pa was eleven years old, he had done a good day's work every day in the fields, driving a team. But Charley did hardly any work at all.

Now Uncle Henry said that Charley must come to the field. He could save them a great deal of time. He could go to the spring for water, and he could fetch them the water-jug when they needed a drink. He could fetch the whetstone when the blades needed sharpening.

All the children looked at Charley. Charley did not want to go to the field. He wanted to stay in the yard and play. But, of course, he did not say so.

Pa and Uncle Henry did not rest at all. They ate in a hurry and went right back to work, and

Charley went with them.

Now Mary was oldest, and she wanted to play a quiet, ladylike play. So in the afternoon the cousins made a playhouse in the yard. The stumps were chairs and tables and stoves, and leaves were dishes, and sticks were the children.

On the way home that night, Laura and Mary heard Pa tell Ma what happened in the field.

Instead of helping Pa and Uncle Henry, Charley was making all the trouble he could. He got in their way so they couldn't swing the cradles. He hid the whetstone, so they had to hunt for it when the blades needed sharpening. He didn't bring the water-jug till Uncle Henry shouted at him three or four times, and then he was sullen.

After that he followed them around, talking and asking questions. They were working too hard to pay any attention to him, so they told him to go away and not bother them.

But they dropped their cradles and ran to him across the field when they heard him scream. The woods were all around the field, and there were snakes in the oats.

When they got to Charley, there was nothing wrong, and he laughed at them. He said:

"I fooled you that time!"

Pa said if he had been Uncle Henry, he would have tanned that boy's hide for him, right then and there. But Uncle Henry did not do it.

So they took a drink of water and went back to work.

Three times Charley screamed, and they ran to him as fast as they could, and he laughed at them. He thought it was a good joke. And still, Uncle Henry did not tan his hide.

Then a fourth time he screamed, louder than ever. Pa and Uncle Henry looked at him, and he was jumping up and down, screaming. They saw nothing wrong with him and they had been fooled so many times that they went on with their work.

Charley kept on screaming, louder and shriller. Pa did not say anything, but Uncle Henry said, "Let him scream." So they went on working and let him scream.

He kept on jumping up and down, scream-ing. He did not stop. At last Uncle Henry said:

"Maybe something really is wrong." They laid down their cradles and went across the field to him.

And all that time Charley had been jumping up and down on a yellow jackets' nest!

The yellow jackets lived in a nest in the ground and Charley stepped on it by mistake. Then all the little bees in their bright yellow jackets came swarming out with their red-hot stings, and they hurt Charley so that he couldn't get away.

He was jumping up and down and hun-dreds of bees were stinging him all over. They were stinging his face and his hands and his neck and his nose, they were crawling up his pants' legs and stinging and crawling down the back of his neck and stinging. The more he jumped and screamed the harder they stung.

Pa and Uncle Henry took him by the arms and ran him away from the yellow jackets' nest.

They undressed him, and his clothes were full of yellow jackets and their stings were swelling up all over him. They killed the bees that were stinging him and they shook the bees out of his clothes and then they dressed him again and sent him to the house.

Laura and Mary and the cousins were playing quietly in the yard, when they heard a loud, blubbering cry. Charley came bawling into the yard and his face was so swollen that the tears could hardly squeeze out of his eyes.

His hands were puffed up, and his neck was puffed out, and his cheeks were big, hard puffs. His fingers stood out stiff and swollen. There were little, hard, white dents all over his puffed-out face and neck.

Laura and Mary and the cousins stood and looked at him.

Ma and Aunt Polly came running out of the house and asked him what was the matter. Charley blubbered and bawled. Ma said it was yellow jackets. She ran to the garden and got a big pan of earth, while Aunt Polly took

Charley into the house and undressed him.

They made a big panful of mud, and plastered him all over with it. They rolled him up in an old sheet and put him to bed. His eyes were swollen shut and his nose was a funny shape. Ma and Aunt Polly covered his whole face with mud and tied the mud on with cloths. Only the end of his nose and his mouth showed.

Aunt Polly steeped some herbs, to give him for his fever. Laura and Mary and the cousins stood around for some time, looking at him.

It was dark that night when Pa and Uncle Henry came from the field. All the oats were in the shock, and now the rain could come and it would not do any harm.

Pa could not stay to supper; he had to get home and do the milking. The cows were already waiting, at home, and when cows are not milked on time they do not give so much milk. He hitched up quickly and they all got into the wagon.

Pa was very tired and his hands ached so that

he could not drive very well, but the horses knew the way home. Ma sat beside him with Baby Carrie, and Laura and Mary sat on the board behind them. Then they heard Pa tell about what Charley had done.

Laura and Mary were horrified. They were often naughty, themselves, but they had never imagined that anyone could be as naughty as Charley had been. He hadn't worked to help save the oats. He hadn't minded his father quickly when his father spoke to him. He had bothered Pa and Uncle Henry when they were hard at work.

Then Pa told about the yellow jackets' nest, and he said:

"It served the little liar right."

After she was in the trundle bed that night, Laura lay and listened to the rain drumming on the roof and streaming from the eaves, and she thought about what Pa had said.

She thought about what the yellow jackets had done to Charley. She thought it served Charley right, too. It served him right because he had been so monstrously naughty. And the bees had a right to sting him, when he jumped on their home.

But she didn't understand why Pa had called him a little liar. She didn't understand how Charley could be a liar, when he had not said a word.

THE WONDERFUL MACHINE

Next day Pa cut the heads from several bundles of the oats, and brought the clean, bright, yellow straws to Ma. She put them in a tub of water, to soften them and keep them soft. Then she sat in the chair by the side of the tub, and braided the straws.

She took up several of them, knotted their ends together, and began to braid. The straws were different lengths, and when she came near the end of one straw, she put a new, long one from the tub in its place and went on braiding.

She let the end of the braid fall back into the

water and kept on braiding till she had many yards of braid. All her spare time for days, she was braiding straws.

She made a fine, narrow, smooth braid, using seven of the smallest straws. She used nine larger straws for a wider braid, and made it notched all along the edges. And from the very largest straws she made the widest braid of all.

When all the straws were braided, she threaded a needle with strong white thread, and beginning at the end of a braid she sewed it round and round, holding the braid so it would lie flat after it was sewed. This made a little mat, and Ma said it was the top of the crown of a hat.

Then she held the braid tighter on one edge, and kept on sewing it around and around. The braid drew in and made the sides of the crown. When the crown was high enough, Ma held the braid loosely again as she kept on sewing around, and the braid lay flat and was the hat brim.

When the brim was wide enough, Ma cut

the braid and sewed the end fast so that it could not unbraid itself.

Ma sewed hats for Mary and Laura of the finest, narrowest braid. For Pa and for herself she made hats of the wider, notched braid. That was Pa's Sunday hat. Then she made him two everyday hats of the coarser, widest braid.

When she finished a hat, Ma set it on a board to dry, shaping it nicely as she did so, and when it dried it stayed in the shape she gave it.

Ma could make beautiful hats. Laura liked to watch her, and she learned how to braid the straw and made a little hat for Charlotte.

The days were growing shorter and the nights were cooler. One night Jack Frost passed by, and in the morning there were bright colors here and there among the green leaves of the Big Woods. Then all the leaves stopped being green. They were yellow and scarlet and crimson and golden and brown.

Along the rail fence the sumac held up its dark red cones of berries above bright flame-colored leaves. Acorns were falling from the oaks, and Laura and Mary made little acorn cups and saucers for the playhouses. Walnuts and hickory nuts were dropping to the ground in the Big Woods, and squirrels were scampering busily everywhere, gathering their winter's store of nuts and hiding them away in hollow trees.

Laura and Mary went with Ma to gather walnuts and hickory nuts and hazelnuts. They spread them in the sun to dry, then they beat off the dried outer hulls and stored the nuts in the attic for winter.

It was fun to gather the large round walnuts and the smaller hickory nuts, and the little hazelnuts that grew in bunches on the bushes. The soft outer hulls of the walnuts were full of a brown juice that stained their hands, but the hazelnut hull smelled good and tasted good, too, when Laura used her teeth to pry a nut loose.

Everyone was busy now, for all the garden vegetables must be stored away. Laura and Mary helped, picking up the dusty potatoes after Pa had dug them from the ground, and pulling the long yellow carrots and the round, purpled-topped turnips, and they helped Ma cook the pumpkin for pumpkin pies.

With the butcher knife Ma cut the big, orange-colored pumpkins into halves. She cleaned the seeds out of the center and cut the pumpkin into long slices, from which she pared the rind. Laura helped her cut the slices into cubes.

Ma put the cubes into the big iron pot on the stove, poured in some water, and then watched while the pumpkin slowly boiled down, all day long. All the water and the juice must be boiled away, and the pumpkin must never burn.

The pumpkin was a thick, dark, good-smelling mass in the kettle. It did not boil like water, but bubbles came up in it and suddenly exploded, leaving holes that closed quickly. Every time a bubble exploded, the rich, hot, pumpkin smell came out.

Laura stood on a chair and watched the pumpkin for Ma, and stirred it with a wooden paddle. She held the paddle in both hands and stirred carefully, because if the pumpkin burned there wouldn't be any pumpkin pies.

For dinner they ate the stewed pumpkin with their bread. They made it into pretty shapes on their plates. It was a beautiful color, and smoothed and molded so prettily with their knives. Ma never allowed them to play with their food at table; they must always eat nicely everything that was set before them, leaving nothing on their plates. But she did let them make the rich, brown, stewed pumpkin into pretty shapes before they ate it.

At other times they had baked Hubbard squash for dinner. The rind was so hard that Ma had to take Pa's ax to cut the squash into pieces. When the pieces were baked in the oven, Laura loved to spread the soft insides with butter and then scoop the yellow flesh from the rind and eat it.

For supper, now, they often had hulled corn and milk. That was good, too. It was so good that Laura could hardly wait for the corn to be ready, after Ma started to hull it. It took two or three days to make hulled corn.

The first day, Ma cleaned and brushed all the ashes out of the cookstove. Then she burned some clean, bright hardwood, and saved its ashes. She put the hardwood ashes in a little cloth bag.

That night Pa brought in some ears of corn with large plump kernels. He nubbed the ears—shelling off the small, chaffy kernels at their tips. Then he shelled the rest into a large pan, until the pan was full.

Early next day Ma put the shelled corn and the bag of ashes into the big iron kettle. She filled the kettle with water, and kept it boiling a long time. At last the kernels of corn began to swell, and they swelled and swelled until their skins split open and began to peel off.

When every skin was loose and peeling, Ma lugged the heavy kettle outdoors. She filled a clean washtub with cold water from the spring, and she dipped the corn out of the kettle into the tub.

Then she rolled the sleeves of her flowered calico dress above her elbows, and she knelt by the tubs. With her hands she rubbed and scrubbed the corn until the hulls came off and floated on top of the water.

Often she poured the water off, and filled the tub again with buckets of water from the spring. She kept on rubbing and scrubbing the corn between her hands, and changing the water, until every hull came off and was washed away.

Ma looked pretty, with her bare arms plump and white, her cheeks so red and her dark hair smooth and shining, while she scrubbed and rubbed the corn in the clear water. She never splashed one drop of water on her pretty dress.

When at last the corn was done, Ma put all the soft, white kernels in a big jar in the pantry. Then, at last, they had hulled corn and milk for supper.

Sometimes they had hulled corn for breakfast, with maple syrup, and sometimes Ma fried the soft kernels in pork drippings. But Laura liked them best with milk.

Autumn was great fun. There was so much work to do, so many good things to eat, so many new things to see. Laura was scampering and chattering like the squirrels, from morning to night.

One frosty morning, a machine came up the road. Four horses were pulling it, and two men were on it. The horses hauled it up into the field where Pa and Uncle Henry and Grandpa and Mr. Peterson had stacked their wheat.

Two more men drove after it another, smaller machine.

Pa called to Ma that the threshers had come; then he hurried out to the field with his team. Laura and Mary asked Ma, and then they ran out to the field after him. They might watch, if they were careful not to get in the way.

Uncle Henry came riding up and tied his horse to a tree. Then he and Pa hitched all the other horses, eight of them, to the smaller machine. They hitched each team to the end of a long stick that came out from the center of the machine. A long iron rod lay along the ground, from this machine to the big machine.

Afterward Laura and Mary asked questions, and Pa told them that the big machine was called the separator, and the rod was called the tumbling rod, and the little machine was called the horsepower. Eight horses were hitched to it and made it go, so this was an eight-horsepower machine.

A man sat on top of the horsepower, and when everything was ready he clucked to the horses, and they began to go. They walked around him in a circle, each team pulling on the long stick to which it was hitched, and following the team ahead. As they went around, they stepped carefully over the tumbling rod, which was tumbling over and over on the ground.

Their pulling made the tumbling rod keep rolling over, and the rod moved the machinery of the separator, which stood beside the stack of wheat.

All this machinery made an enormous racket, rackety-banging and clanging. Laura and Mary held tight to each other's hand, at the edge of the field, and watched with all their eyes. They had never seen a machine before. They had never heard such a racket.

Pa and Uncle Henry, on top of the wheat

stack, were pitching bundles down onto a board. A man stood at the board and cut the bands on the bundles and crowded the bundles one at a time into a hole at the end of the separator.

The hole looked like the separator's mouth, and it had long, iron teeth. The teeth were chewing. They chewed the bundles and the separator swallowed them. Straw blew out at the separator's other end, and wheat poured out of its side.

Two men were working fast, trampling the straw and building it into a stack. One man was working fast, sacking the pouring grain. The grains of wheat poured out of the separator into a half-bushel measure, and as fast as the measure filled, the man slipped an empty one into its place and emptied the full one into a sack. He had just time to empty it and slip it back under the spout before the other measure ran over.

All the men were working as fast as they possibly could, but the machine kept right up with them. Laura and Mary were so excited they could hardly breathe. They held hands tightly and stared.

The horses walked around and around. The man who was driving them cracked his whip and shouted, "Giddap there, John! No use trying to shirk!" Crack! went the whip. "Careful there, Billy! Easy, boy! You can't go but so fast no-how."

The separator swallowed the bundles, the golden straw blew out in a golden cloud, the wheat streamed golden-brown out of the spout, while the men hurried. Pa and Uncle Henry pitched bundles down as fast as they could. And chaff and dust blew over everything.

Laura and Mary watched as long as they could. Then they ran back to the house to help Ma get dinner for all those men.

A big kettle of cabbage and meat was boiling on the stove; a big pan of beans and a johnny-cake were baking in the oven. Laura and Mary set the table for the threshers. They put on salt-rising bread and butter, bowls of stewed pumpkin, pumpkin pies and dried berry pies and cookies, cheese and honey and pitchers of milk.

Then Ma put on the boiled potatoes and cabbage and meat, the baked beans, the hot johnny-cake and the baked Hubbard squash, and she poured the tea.

Laura always wondered why bread made of corn meal was called johnny-cake. It wasn't cake. Ma didn't know, unless the Northern soldiers called it johnny-cake because the people in the South, where they fought, ate so much of it. They called the Southern soldiers Johnny Rebs. Maybe, they called the Southern bread, cake, just for fun.

Ma had heard some say that it should be called journey-cake. She didn't know. It wouldn't be very good bread to take on a journey.

At noon the threshers came in to the table loaded with food. But there was none too much, for threshers work hard and get very hungry.

By the middle of the afternoon the machines had finished all the threshing, and the men who owned them drove them away into the Big Woods, taking with them the sacks of wheat that were their pay. They were going to the next place where neighbors had stacked their wheat and wanted the machines to thresh it.

Pa was very tired that night, but he was happy. He said to Ma:

"It would have taken Henry and Peterson and Pa and me a couple of weeks apiece to thresh as much grain with flails as that machine threshed today. We wouldn't have got as much wheat, either, and it wouldn't have been as clean.

"That machine's a great invention!" he said. "Other folks can stick to old-fashioned ways if they want to, but I'm all for progress. It's a great age we're living in. As long as I raise wheat, I'm going to have a machine come and thresh it, if there's one anywhere in the neighborhood."

He was too tired that night to talk to Laura, but Laura was proud of him. It was Pa who had got the other men to stack their wheat together and send for the threshing machine, and it was a wonderful machine. Everybody was glad it had come.

The Deer in the Wood

The grass was dry and withered, and the cows must be taken out of the woods and kept in the barn to be fed. All the bright-colored leaves became dull brown when the cold fall rains began.

There was no more playing under the trees. But Pa was in the house when it rained, and he began again to play the fiddle after supper.

Then the rains stopped. The weather grew colder. In the early mornings everything sparkled with frost. The days were growing short and a little fire burned all day in the cookstove to keep the house warm. Winter was not far away.

The attic and the cellar were full of good things once more, and Laura and Mary had started to make patchwork quilts. Everything was beginning to be snug and cosy again.

One night when he came in from doing the chores Pa said that after supper he would go to his deer-lick and watch for a deer. There had been no fresh meat in the little house since spring, but now the fawns were grown up, and Pa would go hunting again.

Pa had made a deer-lick, in an open place in the woods, with trees near by in which he could sit to watch it. A deer-lick was a place where the deer came to get salt. When they found a salty place in the ground they came there to lick it, and that was called a deer-lick. Pa had made one by sprinkling salt over the ground.

After supper Pa took his gun and went into the woods, and Laura and Mary went to sleep without any stories or music.

As soon as they woke in the morning they ran to the window, but there was no deer hanging in the trees. Pa had never before gone out to get a deer and come home without one. Laura and Mary did not know what to think.

All day Pa was busy, banking the little house and the barn with dead leaves and straw, held down by stones, to keep out the cold. The weather grew colder all day, and that night there was once more a fire on the hearth and the windows were shut tight and chinked for the winter.

After supper Pa took Laura on his knee, while Mary sat close in her little chair. And Pa said:

"Now I'll tell you why you had no fresh meat to eat today.

"When I went out to the deer-lick, I climbed up into a big oak tree. I found a place on a branch where I was comfortable and could watch the deer-lick. I was near enough to shoot any animal that came to it, and my gun was loaded and ready on my knee.

"There I sat and waited for the moon to rise and light the clearing.

"I was a little tired from chopping wood all day yesterday, and I must have fallen asleep, for I found myself opening my eyes.

"The big, round moon was just rising. I could see it between the bare branches of the trees, low in the sky. And right against it I saw a deer standing. His head was up and he was listening. His great, branching horns stood out above his head. He was dark against the moon.

"It was a perfect shot. But he was so beautiful, he looked so strong and free and wild, that I couldn't kill him. I sat there and looked at him, until he bounded away into the dark woods.

"Then I remembered that Ma and my little girls were waiting for me to bring home some good fresh venison. I made up my mind that next time I would shoot.

"After a while a big bear came lumbering out into the open. He was so fat from feasting on berries and roots and grubs all summer that he was nearly as large as two bears. His head swayed from side to side as he went on all fours across the clear space in the moonlight, until he came to a rotten log. He smelled it, and listened. Then he pawed it apart and sniffed among the broken pieces, eating up the fat white grubs.

"Then he stood up on his hind legs, perfectly still, looking all around him. He seemed to be suspicious that something was wrong. He was trying to see or smell what it was.

"He was a perfect mark to shoot at, but I was so much interested in watching him, and the woods were so peaceful in the moonlight, that I forgot all about my gun. I did not even think of shooting him, until he was waddling away into the woods.

"'This will never do,' I thought. 'I'll never get any meat this way.'

"I settled myself in the tree and waited again. This time I was determined to shoot the next game I saw.

"The moon had risen higher and the moonlight was bright in the little open place. All around it the shadows were dark among the trees.

"After a long while, a doe and her yearling

fawn came stepping daintily out of the shadows. They were not afraid at all. They walked over to the place where I had sprinkled the salt, and they both licked up a little of it.

"Then they raised their heads and looked at each other. The fawn stepped over and stood beside the doe. They stood there together, looking at the woods and the moonlight. Their large eyes were shining and soft.

"I just sat there looking at them, until they walked away among the shadows. Then I climbed down out of the tree and came home."

Laura whispered in his ear, "I'm *glad* you didn't shoot them!"

Mary said, "We can eat bread and butter."

Pa lifted Mary up out of her chair and hugged them both together.

"You're my good girls," he said. "And now it's bedtime. Run along, while I get my fiddle."

When Laura and Mary had said their prayers and were tucked snugly under the trundle bed's covers, Pa was sitting in the firelight with the fiddle. Ma had blown out the lamp because she did not need its light. On the other side of the hearth she was swaying gently in her rocking chair and her knitting needles flashed in and out above the sock she was knitting.

The long winter evenings of fire-light and music had come again.

Pa's fiddle wailed while Pa was singing:

> "Oh, Susi-an-na, don't you cry for me,
> I'm going to Cal-i-for-ni-a,
> The gold dust for to see."

Then Pa began to play again the song about Old Grimes. But he did not sing the words he had sung when Ma was making cheese. These words were different. Pa's strong, sweet voice was softly singing:

> "Shall auld acquaintance be forgot,
> And never brought to mind?
> Shall auld acquaintance be forgot,
> And the days of auld lang syne?
> And the days of auld lang syne, my friend,

And the days of auld lang syne,
Shall auld acquaintance be forgot,
And the days of auld lang syne?"

When the fiddle had stopped singing Laura called out softly, "What are days of auld lang syne, Pa?"

"They are the days of a long time ago, Laura," Pa said. "Go to sleep, now."

But Laura lay awake a little while, listening to Pa's fiddle softly playing and to the lonely sound of the wind in the Big Woods. She looked at Pa sitting on the bench by the hearth, the fire-light gleaming on his brown hair and beard and glistening on the honey-brown fiddle. She looked at Ma, gently rocking and knitting.

She thought to herself, "This is now."

She was glad that the cosy house, and Pa and Ma and the fire-light and the music, were now. They could not be forgotten, she thought, because now is now. It can never be a long time ago.

BEYOND THE PAGES OF

LITTLE HOUSE
IN THE BIG WOODS

Laura Ingalls Wilder was born in the Big Woods of Wisconsin on February 7, 1867, to Charles Ingalls and his wife, Caroline.

When Laura was still a baby, Pa and Ma decided to move to a farm near Keytesville, Missouri, and the family lived there about a year. Then they moved to land on the prairie south of Independence, Kansas. After two years in their little house on the prairie, the Ingallses discovered that the land they lived on belonged to the Osage Indians, so they went back to the Big Woods to live in the same house they had left three years earlier!

This time the family remained in the Big Woods for three years. These were the years that Laura wrote about in her first book, *Little House in the Big Woods*.

In the winter of 1874, when Laura was seven, Ma and Pa decided to move west to Minnesota. They found a beautiful farm near Walnut Grove, on the banks of Plum Creek.

The next two years were hard ones for the Ingallses. Swarms of grasshoppers devoured all the crops in the area, and Ma and Pa could not pay off all their debts. The family decided they could no longer keep the farm on Plum Creek, so they moved to Burr Oak, Iowa.

After a year in Iowa, the family returned to Walnut Grove again, and Pa built a house in town and started a butcher shop. Laura was ten years old by then, and she helped earn money for the family by working in the dining room of the hotel in Walnut Grove, babysitting, and running errands.

The family moved only once more, to the little town of De Smet in Dakota Territory. Laura was now twelve and had lived in at least twelve little houses. Laura grew into a young woman in De Smet, and met her husband, Almanzo Wilder, there.

Laura and Almanzo were married in 1885, and their daughter, Rose, was born in December 1886. By the spring of 1890, Laura and Almanzo had endured too many hardships to continue farming in South Dakota. Their house had burned down in 1889, and their second child, a boy, had died before he was a month old.

First, Laura, Almanzo, and Rose went east to Spring Valley, Minnesota, to live with Almanzo's family. About a year later they moved south to Florida. But Laura did not like Florida, and the family returned to De Smet.

In 1894, Laura, Almanzo, and Rose left De Smet for good and settled in Mansfield, Missouri.

When Laura was in her fifties, she began to write down her memories of her childhood, and in 1932, when Laura was 65 years old, *Little House in the Big Woods* was published. It was an immediate success, and Laura was asked to write more books about her life on the frontier.

Laura died on February 10, 1957, three days after her ninetieth birthday, but interest in the Little House books continued to grow. Since their first publication so many years ago, the Little House books have been read by millions of readers all over the world.

THEN AND NOW

Pa always said, "Other folks can stick to old-fashioned ways if they want to, but I'm all for progress. It's a great age we're living in."

Published in 1932

Published in 1953

Published in 2007

HISTORY

AT THIS TIME IN HISTORY

While Laura and her family were living in the Big Woods from 1871 to 1874 . . .

- Ulysses S. Grant was president of the United States.

- P. T. Barnum opened his circus, which he called "The Greatest Show on Earth," in New York.

- The Great Chicago Fire burned through the city, destroying the town and leaving 90,000 homeless.

- The penny postcard was introduced.

- Susan B. Anthony was fighting for women's voting rights.

- Chewing gum was introduced.

MOLASSES-ON-SNOW CANDY

Before Christmas, Ma spent many hours making good things to eat, including molasses-on-snow candy. Laura and Mary helped Ma make the candy and were allowed to eat one piece each. The rest they saved for Christmas Day, when Aunt Eliza, Uncle Peter, and the cousins came to visit.

To make molasses-on-snow candy, you will need:

1 CUP MOLASSES	*SPOON*
1 CUP BROWN SUGAR	*CANDY THERMOMETER OR*
FRESH CLEAN SNOW	*CUP OF COLD WATER*
(OR FINELY CRUSHED ICE)	*SHALLOW PAN ABOUT 9" X 13"*
MEASURING CUP	*CLEAN TEA TOWEL OR WAXED*
LARGE POT	*PAPER*

1. Mix the molasses and sugar together in the large pot and boil until the mixture reaches the "hard crack" stage on the thermometer or until a drop of the mixture dropped in cold water forms a hard ball and cracks.
2. Remove the syrup from the heat. *Be careful—the syrup is very, very hot!*

3. Scoop fresh, clean snow into the shallow pan. You can also use finely crushed ice, instead of snow.
4. Dribble a spoonful of syrup onto the snow or ice in circles and curlicues and squiggles. Make lots of different shapes.
5. When the syrup turns hard and becomes candy, lift it off the snow and place it on the tea towel or waxed paper to dry.
6. Eat and enjoy!

Song

"Pop! Goes the Weasel"
Words Traditional USA

That night, for a special birthday treat, Pa played "Pop Goes the Weasel" for Laura.

He sat with Laura and Mary close against his knees while he played. "Now watch," he said. "Watch, and maybe you can see the weasel pop out this time."

A penny for a spool of thread,

Another for a needle,

That's the way the money goes—

Pop! goes the weasel!

All around the cobbler's bench,

The monkey chased the weasel,

The preacher kissed the cobbler's wife—

Pop! goes the weasel!

Potatoes for an Irishman's taste,

A doctor for the measles,

A fiddler always for a dance—

Pop! goes the weasel!

Blood pudding for a Dutchman's meal,

A workman for a chisel,

The preacher kissed the cobbler's wife—

Pop! goes the weasel!

From round about the countrymen's barn

The mice began to mizzle,

For when they poke their noses out—

Pop! goes the weasel!

The painter works with ladder and brush,

The artist with the easel,

The fiddler always snaps the strings at—

Pop! goes the weasel!

PLAY HIDE THE THIMBLE

During the dark and cold days of winter, Laura and Mary could not stay outside for long. So they played all kinds of games indoors, including Hide the Thimble. A thimble is a little metal cup that fits on top of your finger when you're sewing. It keeps the needle from hurting your fingertip as you push the needle through the fabric.

To play Hide the Thimble, you will need:
- A thimble (or other small object)
- One or more friends

1. Choose who will hide the thimble first.
2. All the other players close their eyes and count to ten slowly while the thimble hider finds a good spot to hide the thimble.
3. Then the players open their eyes and look for the thimble, while the hider counts to fifty.
4. The first person to find the thimble is the one to hide it next. If no one can find the thimble in time, the same thimble hider hides it again, in a new place.

FARMER BOY

by LAURA INGALLS WILDER

SCHOOL DAYS

It was January in northern New York State, sixty-seven years ago. Snow lay deep everywhere. It loaded the bare limbs of oaks and maples and beeches, it bent the green boughs of cedars and spruces down into the drifts. Billows of snow covered the fields and the stone fences.

Down a long road through the woods a little boy trudged to school, with his big brother Royal and his two sisters, Eliza Jane and Alice. Royal was thirteen years old, Eliza Jane was twelve, and Alice was ten. Almanzo was the youngest of all, and this was his first going-to-school, because he was not quite nine years old.

He had to walk fast to keep up with the others, and he had to carry the dinner-pail.

"Royal ought to carry it," he said. "He's bigger than I be."

Royal strode ahead, big and manly in boots, and Eliza Jane said:

"No, 'Manzo. It's your turn to carry it now, because you're the littlest."

Eliza Jane was bossy. She always knew what was best to do, and she made Almanzo and Alice do it.

Almanzo hurried behind Royal, and Alice hurried behind Eliza Jane, in the deep paths made by bobsled runners. On each side the soft snow was piled high. The road went down a long slope, then it crossed a little bridge and went on for a mile through the frozen woods to the schoolhouse.

The cold nipped Almanzo's eyelids and numbed his nose, but inside his good woolen clothes he was warm. They were all made from the wool of his father's sheep. His underwear was creamy white, but Mother had dyed the wool for his outside clothes.

Butternut hulls had dyed the thread for his coat and his long trousers. Then Mother had woven it, and she had soaked and shrunk the cloth into heavy, thick fullcloth. Not wind nor cold nor even a drenching rain could go through the good fullcloth that Mother made.

For Almanzo's waist she had dyed fine wool as red as a cherry, and she had woven a soft, thin cloth. It was light and warm and beautifully red.

Almanzo's long brown pants buttoned to his red waist with a row of bright brass buttons, all around his middle. The waist's collar buttoned snugly up to his chin, and so did his long coat of brown fullcloth. Mother had made his cap of the same brown fullcloth, with cozy ear-flaps that tied under his chin. And his red mittens were on a string that went up the sleeves of his coat and across the back of his neck. That was so he couldn't lose them.

He wore one pair of socks pulled snug over

the legs of his underdrawers, and another pair outside the legs of his long brown pants, and he wore moccasins. They were exactly like the moccasins that Indians wore.

Girls tied heavy veils over their faces when they went out in winter. But Almanzo was a boy, and his face was out in the frosty air. His cheeks were red as apples and his nose was redder than a cherry, and after he had walked a mile and a half he was glad to see the school-house.